# THE MISUNDERSTANDING OF MISS LOUISA

*School of Charm #2*

MAGGIE DALLEN

Cover by Carpe Librum Book Design

Created with Vellum

# PROLOGUE

Miss Louisa Purchase knew better than to make a sound.

Tiptoeing past her parents' bedroom, and then her elder sister Margaret's, she made her way to the main staircase of their country estate and down to the main hall.

The guests would all be asleep, along with the servants, so really—there was no harm in it.

Besides, her parents might have forbidden her from coming downstairs and joining the revelry the night before, but they had said nothing about the early morning. And it *was* the morning—technically—albeit, very, very early in the morning. Still, she had to assume any pronouncements of not being allowed downstairs *yesterday* were no longer valid.

Obviously, they had not intended for her to stay up in her room *forever*.

She huffed as she clutched her night rail close, padding down the staircase. One silly comment about the fishy smell in the kitchen before the guests had even arrived and she'd been banished forever!

Honestly, what sort of reaction was that? Her parents treated her like a child just because she was not the eldest. Once Margaret married, *then* perhaps she'd be afforded more respect around here...though she was hardly holding her breath. At some point in time she'd been deemed willful and troublesome by her parents, and those types of labels were difficult to shed, she now knew.

No amount of maturation or studious lessons in deportment had rid her of the reputation she'd earned as a small child.

But that was neither here nor there at this particular moment. She'd apologize to her parents for the careless remark later in the day. For the moment, she was the only one awake and her imagination beckoned.

The hallway was empty, as expected. Louisa crept farther along the corridor toward the ballroom, with its high arched ceilings and the shiny wooden floors that almost never got used.

Such a shame.

It was even more of a shame that for once her parents had thrown a proper fete with dancing and music, and *she* had not been invited.

Louisa paused in the doorway with a smile. Some candles were still lit, and the flickering glow bounced off the reflection on the glass doors that led to the balcony. A servant would be along soon, no doubt, to extinguish the candles and tidy up the room, which still looked as though a party had just finished. Even messy and empty, she found herself grinning at the sight of this majestic ballroom.

This room had always made her smile. It was her favorite room in the house, although perhaps it should not have been considering her utter lack of grace.

Five dance instructors over the past few years and she was

no more elegant on the dance floor now as she had been when she used to prance around the nursery.

Perhaps that was why her mother hadn't allowed her to join in the divertissement the night before. She cocked her head to the side as she considered this. It made sense, actually. With the Marquess of Tumberland in attendance and her parents so keen on impressing him, it was no wonder they'd wish to hide Louisa and her terrible dancing skills away.

Well, that and they'd not wish for Margaret to have to compete for attention. Not that anyone feared Louisa would ensnare the marquess with her clever wit or her incomparable beauty... Everyone knew that Louisa, with her fiery red hair and freckles, could not hold a candle to her older sister's fair skin and blonde, curling locks.

But try explaining that to Mother. Or Margaret. Even Father had gotten it into his head that Louisa would be a distraction.

And all because of one silly comment about fish.

Guilt nagged at her. She never had been much good at lying to herself.

She supposed last month's kerfuffle during charades at the Osmond's hunting party had not helped matters. Nor that slip of the tongue when she'd accidentally referred to their youngest daughter by the name of their dog.

In her defense, Louisa never had been much good with names.

Names and dancing and charades—the list of Louisa's failures was growing rapidly and she had a sneaking suspicion that her sister and her parents would be all too happy to add to the list of ways in which Louisa caused chaos. Unintentionally, always, but that did not seem to matter.

Sometimes it seemed to Louisa that she got in trouble for merely existing.

She looked around at the portraits that lined the hallway

outside the ballroom, looking for one familiar face, in particular.

There he was. The dashing Sir Edmond. She sighed as she walked over to him, trailing a finger down the length of his oil-painted chiseled jaw. If Sir Edmond were among the living and not merely haunting this house centuries after his death —she was almost certain he'd have allowed her to dance at the ball.

He wouldn't have hid her away just because a silly marquess was set to arrive and grace them all with his presence.

"You *wouldn't*, would you, Sir Edmond?"

The long-since deceased seafaring warrior frowned down at her as he always did when she spoke to him. That was quite all right. No amount of frowning could hide the glimmer of amusement in his eyes.

Had it been added by the artist?

Perhaps.

But she had no doubt it was based on reality.

Sir Edmond was not related to her by blood—she knew this to be true, his descendants had died out long before her family had taken over this estate. And so she felt perfectly sane for harboring an infatuation for a dead man, no matter what Margaret might say on the matter.

She curtsied before him now, acutely aware of that stirring sensation she always felt when she addressed her dead love. It was the sensation of being watched, though not in a creepy way. He was here with her, she knew it.

Or rather, she did not *know* it. But she still liked to believe it.

This country estate was a lonely place—always had been. Perhaps if she and Margaret had been closer she would not have had to seek out friends with the dead.

But Margaret had not been interested in playing pretend

as a child, and her intense pragmatism had only grown more pronounced as she'd aged. These days Margaret had no interest in any conversation unless it revolved around societal gossip and marriage prospects. She and Mother were so alike in that way, which was lovely for them, she supposed. Not so wonderful for her.

Although—since they had one another, she was often allowed to sit out the never-ending conversations about eligible members of the peerage, and who was the best prospect.

"Perhaps it's for the best, hmm?" she asked Sir Edmond. "Mother and Margaret have each other, and I have you." She beamed at the portrait. "Right, then. Shall we?"

She pretended to take his arm as she headed into the ballroom, curtsying once again as she readied herself for the first dance. A waltz, she decided. Yes, that was exactly what Sir Edmond would wish to dance with her.

Closing her eyes, she allowed her mind to conjure up the music she'd listened to from above the stairs only a few hours earlier. Strains of a beautiful melody played softly in her mind, rising in volume and vigor as the imagined music got underway.

Without stopping to think, her body moved into action. *One, two, three, one, two, three...*

Her eyes still closed, she swayed to the sound of the music in her mind, stepping lightly and without a care now that there were no feet to tread upon.

Sir Edmond was the most gracious partner, as usual. He never minded when she missed a beat or if she got turned about over the steps. Her eyes shut, Louisa could practically feel him smiling down at her, her darling, fierce, enigmatic Sir Edmond.

Imaginary, of course, but that hardly mattered.

And then, quite suddenly—he was not imaginary.

Her breath came to a halt as the air beneath her hands turned solid heat. *Sir Edmond!*

Her eyes flew open and for one startling moment she found herself staring up at the man of her dreams. Light brown hair, chiseled jaw, stern features with a wicked glint of mischief in his eyes.

"Sir Edmond," she breathed.

The gentleman stiffened, his hold on her tightening as his eyes widened, as though *she* were the one startling *him*.

"Er, no." The tight grip on her hand and her waist dropped so quickly she found herself blinking in shock as she tried to process what on earth was happening here.

"*What on earth is happening here*?" Her father's roar had her whipping around to face the now-open balcony doors in time to see her father stepping through along with a handful of other men, only some of whom she recognized.

Her father's expression was livid as he looked from the handsome gentleman beside her to Louisa.

"Oh no," she whispered, her face burning with heat as she realized how this looked.

"What are you doing down here?" her father demanded.

She glanced over at the man who was *not* Sir Edmond. He was staring at her in horrified shock as though *she* were the ghost who'd suddenly sprung to life in his arms and not the other way around.

"I, uh—"

"You're not even dressed," her father pointed out. Helpful, that. Just in case she were not well aware that she was in her nightwear in front of her father's friends and...she glanced over at the handsome man who'd materialized in her arms like the devil himself.

He was eyeing her now from head to toe with a disdainful glare, horror still clear in his eyes.

The stranger and her father's friends all wore matching

looks of scandalized horror. She wrapped her arms around herself. "I, uh, I was—"

Her father didn't wait to hear her answer, whipping around to face the stranger, though his expression lost much of its anger. "What's going on here?"

The man held his hands up in defense as he backed away from her. "I thought she was a child."

What? She swung her head to look at the man. A child. Really. She was nineteen, hardly a *toddler*.

Still, that lame excuse seemed to appease her father, and now he was turning his scowl back to her, looking to her for an explanation as to why she'd been in the arms of a stranger, no doubt.

Her father's accusatory stare rattled her, but not half so much as that disdainful glare from the stranger who'd gotten her into this situation in the first place. Between the two of them, her mind raced and rioted with the unfairness of it all. As such, she did not quite have her wits about her...which was evidenced by the excuse that came tumbling out of her mouth. "I thought he was a ghost!"

This was met by silence all around and Louisa cursed herself for speaking without thinking. She caught a few of the men behind her father exchanging looks of amusement and the embarrassment she'd felt before intensified approximately a million times over.

The stranger seemed to have recovered himself while she burned beside him in abject humiliation. "My apologies, Lord Torrent," he said to her father, irritatingly calm and collected. "I caught sight of your daughter dancing from behind, and I assumed she was a young child."

Louisa glared over at him. Yes, she was short, and perhaps her hair plaited like this made her look more youthful than usual, but still...

She could not help but think that the man who'd just held

her in his arms while her eyes were shut had just sold her down the river.

"I was just dancing," she said to her father. "Minding my own business."

Her father's eyes widened in warning and she fell silent. His voice came out on a low growl. "You were supposed to be upstairs tonight—"

"Yes, but technically it is now morning," she interrupted.

The stranger beside her made an odd choking noise but she dared not drag her gaze from her father's glare to see what he was about.

"You are in your night clothes," her father hissed.

She toyed with the cotton of her nightgown as she gave him a sheepish wince. "I thought everyone was asleep."

Her father glared, the others stared. The man beside her did not move at all.

"Go to your room," her father finally said, his voice so ominous she could not bring herself to say another word. "We shall speak of this in the morning."

Needless to say, she did not point out once again that it was, technically, morning already.

She also did not sleep.

How could she when she knew her father was waiting to give her the lecture of a lifetime for her silly behavior.

She shook her head against her pillow. *So daft*, she mentally scolded herself. Of all the times to anger her father —he'd already been on the war path thanks to her latest scrapes. But this...

She squeezed her eyes shut tight at the memory of his scandalized look. And could she blame him? He'd caught her dancing, alone, in her night rail...with a complete stranger.

She opened her eyes to scowl at the ceiling. Who *was* that man?

And why on earth had he thought it wise to dance with her?

He should have cleared his throat and made his presence known like any normal gentleman would do who'd stumbled upon a lady dancing alone in the wee hours of the morning.

Blasted man with his handsome looks and his mischievous glint.

He'd probably set out to impersonate her beloved Sir Edmond.

She nibbled on her lower lip as she considered that.

All right, fine. Perhaps he had not gone that far. But he *had* sold her out, making it sound like it was all her fault.

*I thought she was a child.*

She scoffed loudly in her bed. Oh please. As if that were some sort of excuse.

*I thought he was a ghost.*

She slammed a pillow over her face to smother her groan. If her father or any of his cohorts had ever doubted her sanity before, they were surely convinced she'd lost her mind now.

If only she could explain...

Maybe she could. Shifting again to try and get comfortable, she told herself that once her father had calmed down, she'd be able to make him see reason.

She would explain everything and *then* he would see. She hadn't been trying to cause trouble.

It had all been a silly misunderstanding.

# 1

S*ix months later...*

Louisa leaned over the edge of the pram. "And so you see, Reggie, it was all just a misunderstanding."

She didn't expect much of an answer from the sleepy babe who stared back at her, so the voice that answered gave her a start.

"Yes, it's all very clear now."

Louisa yelped in surprise and spun around to see her friend Adelaide standing in the doorway grinning. Louisa laughed as she picked a pillow off the bed and hurled it at her friend. "Addie, you scared me half to death!"

"Sorry," Addie said, but she did not look sorry at all. In the months since Addie had come to stay at Lady Charmian's School of Charm, she'd grown into such a different person. She'd gained some much-needed weight and her cheeks were flushed and glowing. More importantly, she was gloriously happy now, where once she'd been so very scared.

And really, who could blame her? The girl's baby brother was safe from the scoundrel who'd tried to kidnap him, she'd found a home and close friends here at the school, and on top of all that—she'd gone and fallen in love with the Earl of Tolston, who adored her beyond all reason.

Really, Addie had gone from desperate runaway to the school's very own fairy tale come to life.

Louisa shifted to look back at Reggie. He might have been Addie's brother, but Louisa and Reggie had formed a bond of their own, and they were fast friends. Reggie's eyes were shutting so she held a finger up to her lips and gestured for Addie to leave the room with her.

Once in the hallway, Louisa linked her arm through Addie's as they headed downstairs for supper. "How much of that did you hear?"

Addie nudged her. "Not enough. I cannot believe you'd tell Reggie the story of how you came to be here at the school before you told me."

Louisa laughed; she knew her friend was in jest. But still, she had a point. Louisa had been awfully stingy with the details of why her parents had sent her away to finishing school, but then again—the other girls were just as quiet about their reason.

The school was meant to teach young ladies to entertain and dazzle in society. Louisa was certain that some of the young ladies here were there for that very reason.

But for Louisa, and some of the others, she suspected, the school had been a convenient place to stash the daughters they did not know what to do with.

"There is not much to tell," Louisa said now as they headed down the steps. "I embarrassed my father one time too many." She held her fingers close together. "I'd come *this close* to being ruined, and that was the last straw." She made a funny face that made Addie laugh. "He thought perhaps this school would help teach me how to stay out of trouble."

*And keep me from embarrassing the family any further.*

"Has it?" Addie's voice was filled with laughter because she knew the answer.

Louisa feigned hurt at the question. "I never needed help on that front, thank you. As I explained to Reggie, that last incident, like all the ones before it, was merely a case of misunderstanding."

Sadly, her father had never given her an opportunity to fully explain that. Before she'd been able to lodge a protest, her father had her bags packed and the carriage called 'round. Tonight, finally, she'd have a chance to explain. Surely by now her father had calmed down enough to see reason. "It really was just a misunderstanding," Louisa said quietly, once more rehearsing what she'd say.

"I see," Addie said. "Because the gentleman in question thought you were a child, and you thought he...was a ghost."

She sighed at her friend's amusement. "Exactly."

Addie patted her arm with a sidelong glance. "I am certain it happens to everyone."

Louisa let out a reluctant laugh at her friend's teasing. Unlike Margaret, Louisa never had been able to take herself all that seriously, and she wasn't about to begin now. "He was more like an apparition, really," she said, her old irritation with the man still there even after six months. She lowered her voice to an ominous whisper. "An evil spirit."

Addie laughed. "Evil, hmm?"

"Undoubtedly. I have no idea how I'd ever managed to confuse him with my dear Sir Edmond, even for one heartbeat."

Addie shook her head. "No, I can imagine. This deceased beau of yours sounds far more congenial."

"Doesn't he, though?"

They were both laughing by the time they reached the dining room. The other girls were already sitting down to eat, and Miss Grayson—the kind unmarried lady who ran the school—greeted them with a warm smile. "Just in time, girls. Have a seat."

Addie leaned over after she sat, her voice quiet so no one else could hear. "I'm dying of curiosity. Who was he?"

Louisa was already distracted by the plate of food a servant offered. "Who was *who*, dear?"

"The mystery man," Addie said. "The gentleman who was *not* deceased and who'd decided to dance with you because—"

"Because he thought I was a child," Louisa finished with a frown. That still rankled. She might not have been the beauty that Margaret was, but she was definitely not a child.

"Yes, him," Addie said. "Who was it?"

Louisa exhaled loudly. She did not wish to speak about the man—the mere memory of him made her surly. And the fact that he would most likely be her brother-in-law in the near future? That made her queasy.

His presence in her life seemed to be unavoidable, which was unbearable to consider. That haughty manner, the high-handed way he'd shifted the blame, not to mention that high-and-mighty glare...

*Insufferable.*

"The Marquess of Tumberland," she mumbled his name under her breath, not wanting to start Prudence or Delilah off on a tangent about eligible young gentlemen this early in the day. Once they got started, there was rarely an end.

"What about Lord Tumberland?" It seemed Delilah had incredibly keen hearing when conversation turned to wealthy marquesses.

"Nothing," Louisa said at the same time Addie spoke.

"Louisa thought he was a ghost."

Louisa grimaced as all eyes turned to her in question. "Only for a moment." Then she smacked Addie's arm, making her friend laugh all over again.

Mercifully, the other girls decided to let the topic drop, no doubt believing it was a silly private joke amongst the two close friends.

"Where have you been all morning, Louisa?" Prudence asked.

Of all the girls here, Prudence was the least likely to ask this. As the resident goody-two-shoes she seemed to have an innate distaste for Louisa. She was always nice enough—she would not be so irritatingly *good* if she were impolite—but the tall girl with the chestnut hair always seemed to address her with pursed lips, as though perhaps she'd just finished sucking on a lemon.

"Yes, we wanted to know what you would be wearing to tonight's festivities," Delilah added as she reached for her glass. The raven-haired beauty arched her perfect brows in a haughty manner, although the more Louisa got to know Delilah the more she realized that the entitled brat persona was just one part of her. The unpleasant part. But when she thought no one was watching, or when she felt one of the girls was in distress, she sometimes—very, *very* rarely—showed a crack in that princess armor, and Louisa was beginning to suspect that somewhere deep, *deep* inside all that gloriously fair skin and jet black hair was a heart of gold.

Not that anyone would admit that aloud—most certainly not Delilah.

Addie leaned over to Louisa in eager excitement. "Oh yes, please say you'll be joining us this evening."

"*I* plan on wearing my blue gown," Delilah said, not bothering to glance over as she made this announcement. "If you are joining, do not even think about wearing yours."

Louisa met Miss Grayson's gaze across the table and they

shared a small smile at Delilah's expense. Louisa's mother had sent a blue gown last month and it just so happened to bear a resemblance to Delilah's.

It had nearly meant the end of the rather odd, entirely singular, and exquisitely fragile new alliance amongst the girls of this house. Ever since Addie's ordeal had been exposed and she'd been attacked in their own home weeks before, the girls had formed a truce. Maybe even a friendship.

After a lifetime of being on her own, Louisa wouldn't dream of letting a silly gown ruin that.

Miss Grayson, who knew this very well, answered on her behalf. "You have nothing to fear, Delilah. Louisa sent the gown to the modiste and had her gown dyed a different color."

Delilah shot her a look of surprise and Louisa shrugged. "Blue has never been my color anyway."

This earned her a small, almost grudging smile from Princess Delilah, as Louisa had started to think of her.

"You haven't answered the question," Prudence pointed out. "Will you be joining us at the Havershams for the musicale?"

The Havershams were relatives of Addie and Reggie. While they'd offered to take Addie in once they learned of her true identity, Addie had opted to stay here where she felt like she had a home.

A boon for Louisa, to be sure. She'd be missing Addie and Reggie terribly when they finally did leave. Though there was no doubt, Addie's next home would be with the Earl of Tolston, and she'd been assured by both Addie and Tolston that she would always be welcome.

"A musicale, hmm?" she asked, turning to face Addie. "Might I assume this is another occasion for Lord Tolston to swoon over you?"

The other girls giggled as Addie blushed. "Perhaps," she said with an adorably smug smile.

Louisa laughed. "Well, much as I hate to miss watching my two favorite lovebirds gaze longingly at one another, I am afraid I shall have to miss it."

"Do you have other plans?" Prudence asked.

Louisa nodded, hoping her smile wasn't fading on her as nerves took hold. "My family is in town for the remainder of the season. They've only just arrived and would like for me to stop by for a visit."

This was...not quite a lie. It was not entirely the truth either. But to say 'my family is in town and expressed no interest in seeing me' sounded too depressing for her own ears. Definitely not something she needed to share with others.

Besides, she was certain her mother and sister wished to see her—they were just not terribly effusive in their correspondence, that was all. But her mother had mentioned they'd be staying in tonight, and while that was hardly an invitation—a daughter didn't need an invitation to sup with her own family. Everyone knew that.

She was certain they would be happy to see her when she came to dinner. It would be a surprise.

And really, who didn't enjoy a good surprise?

# 2

"Tell me again why we are dining with the Viscount of Torrent and his family?" Mr. Gregory Allen asked.

Lawrence Rivulet, the Marquess of Tumberland, turned from looking out the window to see his friend from Eton lounging in his seat looking far worse for the wear after last night's debaucherous evening at a gaming hell. "You did not have to join me, you know."

Gregory grinned. Even in his rough state, the younger man still looked happier than Lawrence had ever managed being on his best of days. "It was either this or get dragged along to a musicale with my cousin."

"I thought you got on well with Tolston," Lawrence said.

"Indeed, I do. But much as I enjoy watching the old man giddy and in love, even *I* draw the line at musicales. They bore me to tears."

Lawrence smirked. "They must be very dull, indeed, if dining with the viscount's family sounds more enjoyable."

"Are you joking?" Gregory laughed. "They have a daughter

who prances around with ghosts in her nightgown. They sound far more entertaining."

Lawrence scowled over at his longtime friend. "I told you that in confidence."

"And I have said naught to a soul," Gregory said quickly.

Lawrence huffed. "Then how is it I have heard whispers about that poor girl."

*I thought he was a ghost!* The memory of that night still made his lips twitch with mirth, even now, so many months later.

It had been the most novel evening he could remember. Well, the evening up until that moment had been deadly dull, but there was nothing like a near-scandal with a pretty young lady in a nightgown to liven a situation.

"You were not the only one in attendance," Gregory reminded him. "Someone else must have talked."

He grunted in acknowledgment, vowing right then and there to give hell to whomever it was who'd spread the gossip about him and the young lady.

The gossip wasn't bad enough to ruin the poor lass, but it was enough to cause a stir, and no gossip was good gossip when it came to sweet, innocent debutantes and the *ton*.

He shifted in his seat uncomfortably. It was regret, no doubt, that fed his determination to do right by the girl now, when he'd done such a bad job of it that night.

In his defense, he'd been too taken aback by the oddity of the situation to do more than stammer a defense for his own actions. The moment he'd realized his mistake, he'd been beset by shock and horror. The implications of what he'd done—of what he had appeared to have done...

"Much as I'd love to meet the daft girl, I thought you weren't terribly fond of the viscount and his family." Gregory held up a finger. "Enchanting midnight dancers aside, that is."

Lawrence fought a grin and lost. *Enchanting*, that was one word for the redhead with the big green eyes and the fetching freckles. He rubbed a hand over his face, wiping away the smile. "I'm not terribly keen on them but they own the property next to mine and rumor has it, he's looking to sell a portion of his estate."

"Rumor has it he is bankrupt," Gregory said bluntly.

Lawrence dipped his head in acknowledgement. "That too."

"So, he is looking for you to buy his land?" he asked.

"It would appear that way," he hedged.

"Are you interested in buying the land?" Gregory asked.

He shrugged. "If we can come to an agreeable arrangement."

"Hmmph." Gregory regarded him steadily. "Would this arrangement involve you marrying his daughter?"

Lawrence's mind automatically called up bright red hair and equally red cheeks. "What? No. Of course not."

Gregory held his hands up. "No need to get worked up, old chap. I'm just drawing logical conclusions. You are neighbors, they are a good family—minus one odd black sheep," he added with a wicked grin. "Word is the eldest daughter is quite pretty."

"Mmm." Lawrence honestly had nothing else to say on the matter, not because he disagreed, only because...he could not remember. He had a vague memory of blonde hair and a simpering smile during the soiree he'd attended at their country estate months earlier. But, for the life of him, he could not recall if they had talked and, if so, what they'd discussed.

Truth be told, the only vivid memory he carried from that night was the unexpected sight of a redhead dancing, which had been followed closely by the startling shock of realizing he'd made a massive mistake.

Lawrence dropped his head back against the seat with a sigh. If he could turn back time, he'd do it all over again.

This time, when he walked into the supposedly empty ballroom to snatch up the last of his drink, he'd take one look at the ethereal vision floating across the floor and then he would run.

That's what he should have done.

Instead, he'd stood there like a fool, watching her.

Whether it was the alcohol in his system, or the dim candlelight, or the way her hair had fallen down her back in a long braid, or the way she was padding around barefoot... He'd gotten it into his head that she was a child. Some delightfully enchanting young girl dancing clumsily as she spoke to her make-believe partner.

He should have waited until she'd spun around so he could see her face, not to mention the soft swell of her curves, which were unabashedly clear when he'd viewed her face-to-face a little later.

But instead of doing anything right, he'd taken one look, decreed her a child, and had thought to make her laugh by dancing with her.

He had *not* made her laugh.

Indeed, he was fairly certain he'd ruined her night, her father's good favor, and any chance that he might have had of walking away from her father's pleas to buy his land.

It was one thing to turn away from a neighbor who'd fallen on hard times. It was quite another to turn one's back on the man who'd forgiven him for embracing his scantily clad daughter. Alone, no less. And in the middle of the night.

"What's that sigh for?" Gregory asked.

Lawrence opened his eyes just as the carriage slowed on a quiet, tree-lined street. "Just that I'm fairly certain this deal is done, whether I want it or not. I'm hardly in a position to argue when the viscount forgave me so easily for that ridiculous debacle."

Gregory laughed. "Do you think he forgave his daughter so easily?"

Lawrence winced at the memory of her expression in the face of her father's rage. "I'm sure he got over it in time," he said.

Not that he'd been of any help.

It was guilt, plain and simple, that had him hoping she'd be there tonight so he could see for his own eyes how well she'd recovered after that night.

Lawrence leaned forward in his seat to try and catch sight of the townhouse the viscount had rented for the season. A new eagerness had him itching to open the carriage door the moment it came to a stop.

"My, my," Gregory drawled. "Are you so very eager to attend a dull dinner party...or to see viscount's beautiful daughter?"

Lawrence glared over at his friend. "I'm not here for the girl," he started, even as his mind rushed to envision what the bright-eyed redhead looked like with her hair up and wearing a gown—

"I wouldn't blame you in the least," Gregory said quickly. "Like I said, Miss Margaret is said to be quite the beauty."

*Margaret.* He stared at his friend in confusion for a moment. Then once again he had a vague image of blonde hair and an ever-present smile.

Ah yes. Margaret.

"I am not here for Margaret," he said.

Gregory's smile turned irritatingly annoying.

"Or any other young ladies who happen to be here."

"Whatever you say," Gregory murmured.

Lawrence leaned forward to open the carriage door when it came to a halt, but turned quickly to jab a finger in his friend's face. "Whatever you do, do not go in here making insinuations to embarrass the poor girl. She's already been through enough."

Gregory's eyes widened. "I would not dream of it."

Just as Lawrence was turning away, Gregory mumbled, "Besides, I hear she's only interested in dead men, anyway."

# 3

Louisa had to admit, she'd expected her family to be *slightly* more enthusiastic at the sight of her. Instead, they were eyeing her in the drawing room like she was some sort of puzzle.

"So you just...decided to visit," her mother said, trying and failing, it seemed, to grasp the situation. Her brows were knit in confusion as though this was truly a stunning turn of events.

"That's right." Louisa's smile never faltered. "You'd said you would be staying in this evening and so—"

"You told her that?" Her father addressed her mother, making it sound like an accusation.

"Yes, well..." Her mother clutched at her pearls. "I did not realize she would take that as an invitation."

Louisa—the *she* in question—tried not to be hurt. Truly she did. Clearly surprising her family had not been the best tactic. She glanced over at her sister and received a tepid smile in response. Not exactly a warm welcome but better than anything her mother and father had managed to muster.

Looking at the three of them, standing there like some

fair-haired portrait of domestic bliss, she felt more like an outsider than she cared to admit. The odd man out, that was she. Flaming red hair while they were blond, short and curvy where they were tall and willowy, loud and prone to sticking her foot in her mouth where they were quiet and dignified...

The list went on and on, really.

"You needn't worry," she said, aiming for a teasing tone. "If there is not enough food to spare, I shall be just fine with a bit of bread and cheese."

Silence.

Her smile started to feel strained. Her cheeks ached with the effort to pretend that her feelings weren't hurt by this cold reception.

Margaret was the first to break it by stepping forward and embracing her stiffly. "It *is* good to see you, Lulu."

The use of her old nickname gave her a much needed dose of warmth. She and Margaret had never been close, but this was still her sister, and her sister truly was kind at heart. Too kind to let Louisa feel unwelcome.

"Of *course* you are welcome." Her mother's smile looked strained, her gaze flustered as she looked from Louisa to her husband and back again.

Louisa too turned her gaze to her father. It was true they had not parted on the best terms when she'd last seen him, but he was her father and he loved her. She knew this to be true.

He seemed to remember it at the same time as she and the hard lines of his face creased into a rueful smile. "Louisa, you know you are always welcome with your family..."

He trailed off.

A 'however' seemed to hang quietly in the air amongst them. Another awkward exchange of looks between her parents and her sister.

Her mother turned to face her with a grimace. "It is just

that...this particular evening is perhaps not the best time for a visit."

"Any other evening," her sister added quickly, her brows high with an optimistic look that fooled no one. Least of all Louisa.

She was not wanted here.

Louisa's throat swelled, her chest ached. But her smile grew more brilliant than ever with false cheer. "I see," her voice was too breathy but she managed to sound upbeat. "I understand completely."

She did not understand. Not at all. But her pride was stinging and she hated the glimpses of pity she caught from her sister, her mother...even her father.

"I will just, uh..." Too late she realized that she'd sent away the school's carriage. It had not occurred to her that she might need to flee her family's home on such short notice.

How thoughtless of her.

Her father seemed to understand her predicament. "I shall have Mrs. Martin escort you home."

*Home.* Her eyes stung but she widened them farther, not wanting her father to see how much it hurt that he'd referred to a finishing school as her home. *Is my home not here with you?*

She bit back the question because the answer was clear.

No. Apparently not.

"I will have the carriage brought around," her father said, moving toward the door of the drawing room with rare speed.

"I shall go tell Mrs. Martin to be ready," her mother said, off to find their long-time housekeeper.

And then Louisa was alone with Margaret, the beloved daughter. The great blonde hope for a good match. The daughter who did not cause scandals wherever she went and who never once embarrassed their parents—accidentally or otherwise.

"Well, I hope you enjoy your evening," Louisa managed,

already moving to follow her parents to let them know there was no need to bring her ride around. She could go to the carriage house on her own. She could slink out the back like a burglar or a thief.

"Wait," Margaret said, her voice a little too loud.

Louisa paused in the doorway.

"Please, do not leave like this," Margaret said.

Kind, noble Margaret. She was twisting her gloved hands together in agitation when Louisa turned to face her. She looked prettier than ever, Louisa noticed. She was wearing a shimmering new gown that suited her willowy figure, and her hair was done in an intricate design. Standing there in the middle of the room alone, with her hands clasped demurely—Margaret looked like perfection.

Louisa was reminded of a doll she'd received as a present when she was a child—the thing had been so delicate, so dainty, so *perfect.* Not a hair out of place. It's porcelain skin unblemished...

Until Louisa got her hands on it.

Louisa had wrecked that doll, and she had a feeling she was being sent away now so she could not do the same to Margaret.

Her sister looked pained now—filled with regret because of course Louisa had not done a decent job of hiding her hurt.

Margaret would have been able to hide her pain.

Louisa never had learned how to do that.

"It is all right, Margaret," she said with a small smile. "I understand."

Margaret finally broke her perfect pose and hurried over to her. "I do not think that you do, Lulu."

Louisa huffed. Her nickname had been a nice reminder of their familial bond just a moment ago, but now it spoke to her being the younger sister. It made her feel like a child. She sniffed and tilted her chin up. "Then why don't you explain it to me?"

Margaret's expression grew strained as she looked from Louisa to the door where their parents had just left. "They need me to make a good match, you know that."

Louisa nodded. This was hardly news. All anyone had been talking about since Margaret made her debut last season was how wonderful a match she was sure to make.

Granted, she hadn't yet, but that didn't stop everyone from fussing over Margaret, praising her constantly for being such an elegant and poised young lady, not to mention such a beauty.

Margaret licked her lips. "You don't understand, Louisa." She narrowed her eyes slightly, meaningfully. "They *need* me to make a good match."

Louisa blinked as her words took on a new meaning. "Are you saying..." She inhaled sharply, her brain putting pieces together to form a whole new picture. "Does this mean..."

Margaret regarded her steadily, waiting for her to catch up. The short season this year, the rented townhouse because theirs had been sold, the noticeable lack of staff these past few years, the dinner parties and soirees last year at which her father spent most of the time locked in an office with the other gentlemen.

It all came back to her at once and the individual memories seemed to collide together. The pieces of a puzzle forming a whole picture at last.

Louisa met Margaret's gaze evenly. "How bad is it?"

Margaret's expression was so strained, her lips pressed tight together as she shrugged. "Honestly, I do not know. I only know what I've overheard or pieced together."

Louisa nodded, her insides deflating oddly with guilt and shame. How had Margaret gleaned that her parents were facing financial difficulties when she had not?

A whole new thought occurred to her as she heard servants bustling about in the other room. "You have guests this evening," she said, stating the obvious.

Margaret nodded, her gaze holding hers steadily.

"Who is it?"

"The Marquess of Tumberland and his friend."

Louisa bit her lip, a surge of heat creeping into her cheeks at the mere mention of his name. She'd heard countless times that he would be the ideal match for Margaret, but now those words, which had seemed like idle gossip at the time, took on a new significance.

"Is he courting you?" Louisa blurted out.

Now it was Margaret's turn to blush and she glanced around the room as if gossipmongers might be hiding behind the credenza. "No, Lulu," she said, her voice resigned. "Not yet, at least."

Louisa caught a flicker of determination in her sister's eyes and her own eyes widened in surprise. She'd heard her sister talk about eligible men for years now, but she'd never seen this side of her before. She looked resigned. Determined, even.

It was...impressive, really.

"Do you like him?" Louisa asked.

"Louisa, please." Margaret said this with an exasperated huff, as though the question were ridiculous.

For what felt like the millionth time this year alone, Louisa got the sense that she and her sister were speaking different languages. Louisa felt that liking one's intended was rather pertinent, indeed.

But clearly Margaret was more focused on marrying to save their coffers, and *that* Louisa had to admire even if she could not quite comprehend it.

She'd always thought her sister was merely obsessed with gaining status and riches and running her own house, but she was starting to think that perhaps she'd been judging Margaret too harshly.

Worse, she was starting to understand that perhaps *she* was the selfish one in this family. She bit her lip as a surge of shame had tears stinging the back of her eyes all over again. "I've never meant to be an embarrassment," she said in a high, tight voice.

Margaret sighed and her smile was weary. "I know, dear. We all know that. You're just..." She flailed a hand. "You are *you*."

Louisa let out a choked laugh, one that sounded like a sputter and a sneeze at once. It was the sort of sound Margaret would never make, not even in private, and just one more reminder of how badly Louisa represented her family.

Well, no more.

Louisa straightened her shoulders. She would just have to change, that was all. There was no time like the present to start fresh and make a new name for herself. She was currently living at a finishing school, for heaven's sake. There could be no better place for her right now.

"I wish I could do something to help," she said.

Margaret reached out and squeezed her hand. "I did not mean to make you fret, Lulu. I just wanted to explain why we acted the way we did when you showed up here so unexpectedly."

Louisa nodded, her chest still aching with humiliation and shame, but at least now she understood why she'd not been wanted. If there was anyone who could ruin the marquess's good opinion of Margaret and this family...it was she.

Louisa cringed at the memory of their one and only meeting. He must think her a lunatic...or a child.

Or both.

Ugh, was it any wonder they wanted her far, far away from

tonight's visitors? Especially when Margaret was looking so lovely and Louisa was—

"They are here!" Her mother rushed into the room with more frantic haste than Louisa had ever seen her exhibit before. Which honestly, wasn't much. Even in a tizzy, her mother kept her composure. Just like Margaret.

Too bad Louisa hadn't seemed to inherit any of that innate grace and poise.

Louisa held back a sigh. There would be plenty of time for self-pity when she was back at the school, comfortable and cozy with Reggie and the housekeeper while the other girls enjoyed an evening at the musicale.

At least there she had Reggie, and it was nearly impossible to get into trouble.

She headed over to Margaret and gave her a quick squeeze. Two hugs in one evening was a new record for the Purchase girls, but this was a night of new understandings. Her sister was acting on behalf of the family, and Louisa would do anything she could to help.

Right now that meant leaving, and not reminding the mighty marquess of the odd little sister who darkened the family's good name. "Good luck," she whispered to her sister.

Margaret gave her a tight smile and they both started when their father came bounding into the room, buzzing with energy. *Nervous* energy.

Her father was nervous. Scared, even.

Louisa felt it to her core, and had to clench her fists at her sides to keep from running over to her father and wrapping her arms around his neck. A selfish part of her was desperate to apologize for adding to his troubles, and a daughterly love made her want to comfort him in whatever way she could.

She sniffed as she headed toward the door of the drawing room with new determination. This was the dawn of a new day. She was officially saying goodbye to her own selfish, childish desires, and embracing her new role in this family.

She lifted her chin as she reached her father. "I will leave, Father, and I will ensure that Lord Tumberland never sees me."

Her father's brows hitched up in surprise—no doubt at her very serious tone. This was a new side of her he'd never seen, but he would have to get used to it. She clapped a hand on his shoulder as she passed. "I wish you all the best this evening."

"Er...thank you, Louisa."

She could not blame him for being confused by her behavior. He had yet to experience this new and improved, serious, polished, docile, and oh-so-mature Louisa. But soon he would know her well.

He started to follow her, but she flashed him a reassuring smile. "I shall see myself out. You must see to your guests."

"Oh, uh...all right then."

In the hallway, she headed toward the servants' entrance in the back. There was no way she would risk running into the marquess and his friend by going out the front door.

There was a bustle of activity going on in the back of the house as the servants prepared for this monumental dinner. She greeted the servants she recognized, stopping briefly to introduce herself to the ones she did not know. By the time she reached the back entrance, she was certain she could slip away without being seen...

Until she saw it. The vat of hot water that was currently blocking her escape.

"Apologies, my lady," the cook said. "I'll have Johnny move it shortly."

And interfere with the industrious activity that would ensure a smooth and orderly meal? She thought not. "No need, I shall find another way out."

"I've had the groomsman bring the carriage around to the side of the house as your father requested," the butler informed as she passed.

Excellent. The side of the house was ideal—little more than an alley in which she could skulk off like a thief in the night.

She fought a grin. This was a serious matter, after all. Not an adventure. Certainly not.

And yet her heart was thudding loudly in her chest at the excitement of trying to escape. She could hear voices in the main hallway, her family gathering to greet their visitors, no doubt.

A little exploration showed that she could either go back the way she'd come or climb out through the study window, which led directly to the alley.

The voices grew louder as servants rushed past her toward the front door.

Her heart leapt with the danger of it all. The excitement!

No, not the excitement. She was a dutiful daughter, that was all. And no one would want her to reappear at the front entrance *now*—not when the marquess would be entering at any moment.

She glanced out the window—not a bad jump, really. Louisa stood back and brushed her hands on her skirt as she prepared to hoist the window. No, not a bad jump at all. She could handle it easily.

Besides, this was what a dutiful daughter would do.

# 4

"You know, we *could* turn back," Gregory said as he and Lawrence loitered in front of the townhouse, making no move to knock.

"Don't be ridiculous," Lawrence said, although the idea was not at all off-putting. In fact, it was rather enticing. He wasn't in the mood to be polite and listen to idle, boring chatter.

He was not in the mood to be *bored,* in fact, and that was the crux of it. These days boredom seemed to plague him wherever he went. Every dinner, every ball, every evening spent at his club—they all blended together these days.

Maybe that was a sign he was getting old.

He wasn't old *yet*, obviously. He was still young, physically speaking. It was in every other way that he felt ancient.

Only one memory stuck out of late. The memory of a silly redheaded young lady who'd declared him a ghost.

The memory had his lips twitching with amusement and he eyed the front door with a little less abhorrence. There was every chance she would be there. She was one of Torrent's daughters, of course she'd be there.

"Let's get this over with," he said to Gregory.

"That's the spirit, my friend." Gregory started forward, all eager enthusiasm.

Lawrence was slower to fall behind. The thought of the younger sister was enticing, no doubt, but that didn't make the prospect of business discussions and a tediously long dinner sound any more appealing.

He'd just hit the front steps when he heard it.

A squeaking sound coming from the alley beside the house. The squeak was followed by a grunt.

What on earth?

"One moment, Gregory," he called up to his friend.

Gregory gave him a jaunty salute and leaned against the doorframe to await him as he hurried around the corner. Another squeaking noise. Was that a *meow*?

He furrowed his brow as he stared into the shadows of the narrow alley. He might have a reputation for being standoffish and too serious but that didn't mean he had no heart. He never had been able to abide the thought of an innocent animal being hurt.

He picked up his pace, his attention caught by a movement just over his head. A window. He stared in disbelief until he was right under the window.

This was...*not* a cat.

It still took another heartbeat to make out what it was, however.

White fabric billowed and bloomed overhead, and then a leg shot out with an *oof*.

It was a lady. Why on earth...? Oh, what did it matter why? There was a damsel in distress straddling a windowsill.

"Pardon me, are you all right?" he called up. "Do you need assis—"

The woman above him squeaked and jerked at the sound of his voice. And then—

*Oof.*

She fell on him.

He made a valiant attempt to keep the lady from danger, clutching her to his chest as they both toppled to the ground. His body taking the brunt of the fall.

"Oh my heavens," a female voice atop him said, her voice breathless and winded—though no doubt not quite as winded as he. He struggled to draw in a deep breath as the young lady shifted aside, falling onto her bottom beside him with another *oof.*

Silence fell. The kind of silence that seems to echo because it is so stunningly quiet after a moment of such violent upheaval.

It was the kind of silence befitting this moment when a woman had toppled out of a window and brought them both to the ground.

"I'm so sorry," the lady in question said, breaking the silence in a flurry of movements.

Stunned, Lawrence watched in fascination as the redhead from his most vivid memory ran her hands over his shoulders and his chest. Feeling for...what?

He had no idea.

But he did not want her to stop.

"Are you all right?" Her worried gaze rose to meet his and she froze.

*He* froze.

They stared at one another for an interminable moment and he watched as her eyes filled with recognition, followed by shock, followed by...

*Horror.*

"Oh no." She scrambled backwards on her hands and feet like a crab until her foot caught on her skirt and her bottom landed on the ground with a thud.

Again.

She clamped her mouth shut just as he caught his breath... and found his voice. "What on earth were you doing?"

She winced and he realized it had come out rather loudly. But then again...what *on earth* had she been *doing*?

She straightened, her chin going up high as anger flashed in her eyes. "What are you doing back here?"

He threw a hand out to the opening from which she'd just arrived. "You came out of a window!"

"And you were loitering in an alley!"

Her chest rose and fell with her quick breaths, and he had the most insane urge to laugh.

He rarely laughed.

He also had another uncharacteristic desire, but it was vastly more ridiculous. He had the urge to lean over, tug her into his arms and kiss her.

Ridiculous, he told himself. But now he was the one who suffered from labored breathing.

*Focus, Tumberland.*

She recovered first, crossing her arms and looking absurdly dignified for someone who'd just toppled out of a window. "I needed air," she said stiffly. She narrowed her eyes. "Why were you in an alley?"

"I was just waiting for a lady to fall into my arms."

She huffed, her glare unwavering as her lips pinched at his sarcasm.

"I thought I heard an animal in distress," he said.

"An *animal*?" Her indignation was something to see. Her eyes flashed with pride, and her shoulders thrust back. "It was not an animal."

"Yes, so I've noticed. But, you see, I thought I heard a cat—"

"A *cat*?" Her voice went high-pitched at that.

"In distress," he continued, oddly enchanted by the sight of her outrage.

"You thought you heard a cat in a distress and you...what? Just chased after it?" Her gaze met his. "Well, that's..." He saw the moment his words registered and she heard what she'd said. "That's awfully thoughtful of you, actually."

She muttered it softly. Reluctantly.

He found himself fighting a smile. "Yes, well, I have my moments."

Her anger seemed to be fading fast. Maybe now he could get through to her. Make her talk. Because he had questions of his own and he wasn't going anywhere until he got answers. "Miss Purchase—"

"It's Miss Louisa," she said.

"Miss Louisa, why on earth were you climbing out of a window? And please do not try and convince me that the air in this alley was what drove you to it."

They both inhaled and he was certain she smelled the unsavory scents from the street just as well as he.

"Very well, I was—" She clamped her mouth shut as her cheeks grew rosy. "Uh, that is, I was trying to..."

She stopped talking. He waited just long enough until it was clear she was done. That was the only explanation she was going to offer.

"Ah, I see," he said. "That explains everything."

She blinked in the face of his sarcasm. He was used to that response. Meanwhile, he was taking her in. All of her. She'd righted her skirts but he found himself cataloging every freckle, every stray hair—of which there were many thanks to that tumble—and every dirt smudge on her gloves. Concern temporarily overrode curiosity. "Are you all right?"

"Yes." Then she mashed her lips together, and he got the feeling she was trying to keep from speaking.

The attempt looked painful.

He arched a brow, and she caved. "It seems someone broke my fall." She clamped her mouth shut once more but not before he caught the tiniest hitch of her lips. She was trying not to laugh.

The little minx.

He narrowed his eyes. "Yes, it seems I have excellent timing."

She shut her eyes for a moment and drew in a deep breath. "My lord, I am so very sorry—"

He held up a hand to silence her. "I do not need your apologies." He dropped his hand. "It is my honor to break a lady's fall."

He'd been told before that he had a dry sense of humor. Some might say it was dry bordering on nonexistent. Most did not know whether he was, in fact, in jest.

This was not the case with Louisa. She burst out in an adorably genuine laugh. Short, loud, and just shy of a cackle. Then she slapped a hand over her mouth to stifle it and once again he caught her closing her eyes briefly and taking a deep breath.

"Are you attempting to calm yourself?" He was honestly curious. The girl's emotions seemed to be all over the place and it was impossible to read how she might react next. One moment she was painfully embarrassed, the next she was trying not to tease him, and then she *laughed.*

At his joke.

No one ever laughed at his jokes.

He was beyond flummoxed by the whole situation. So much so, he didn't move to get off the ground or offer his hand to bring her to her feet.

Oddly enough, she seemed just as content to stay there as well. Like they'd both just decided to have a picnic in an alley. As one does.

Her eyes fluttered open. "I apologize, my lord—"

"What did I say about apologies?"

She bit her lip. "You're right. I'm sorr—" She caught

herself with a funny little wince. Letting out a long exhale, she said, "It is just that sometimes when I am in a predicament, it is difficult for me not to laugh."

"I see." He studied her and found her green eyes wide with sincerity. *Adorable*. "And do you often find yourself in such a...predicament?" He gestured to their little picnic to make his point.

"Not precisely like this but...yes," she said with a weary sigh that nearly made him laugh aloud. Now it was his turn to fight for composure and he felt certain he could say with no qualms that he had never in his life had to battle for composure.

This girl had an odd effect. He shifted, bringing one leg in so he could better face her. "First I find you dancing in the middle of the night—"

"Early morning," she interrupted, catching that full lower lip of hers with her teeth the moment his gaze cut to hers.

"You are correct. My apologies," he said. "I caught you dancing alone in your nightgown in the early morning, and now...this."

She hung her head and mumbled something to herself that he did not quite hear. Whatever it was, her entire demeanor shifted once again. The humor and embarrassment faded to something morose that had his own heart clenching in response.

He tried to make his tone gentle and sensitive. "Were you running away?"

"No!" Her head shot up quickly. "Of course not. I was merely heading back home."

"This is not your home?" he asked. For the life of him, he couldn't quite seem to catch up with this conversation.

"Apparently not." There was no denying the hint of sadness in her tone as she mumbled it, her gaze on the ground.

"I see." He most definitely did *not* see.

"So, if you were not running away from home," he started slowly, hoping that perhaps she might jump in with some sort of clue to help him along.

She did not.

She merely lifted her gaze to meet his, her brows arching slowly as if she too was wondering what he might guess next.

He cleared his throat. "Why didn't you just walk out the front door?"

She licked her lips. "Well, uh, you see..." There was that blush again. It made her green eyes sparkle like jewels. The pink in her cheeks matched the color of her lips, and if she kept biting her bottom lip like that it would grow even more swollen and even more...*kissable.*

"Tumberland, you back there?" Gregory's voice just around the corner had him shaking his head, once more back in reality.

The same seemed to happen to the girl with the fiery hair because her eyes went wide as she scrambled to her feet. "Oh, please, don't let him come back here."

"It's all right, Gregory. I'll be right there," he called to his friend. "Where do you think you're going?"

She was scurrying toward the back of the alley. Who knew what was back there?

"I need to get back," she said quickly. "I am truly sorry."

"If you apologize again, I shall never forgive you," he said.

She laughed. He smirked. He liked that she understood when he was teasing.

She stopped at the back of the alley. "I...I know I cannot ask you any favors but—"

"Go on, ask," he said. His curiosity was piqued, that was all. That was the only reason he wanted her to stay and talk to him. Ask him a favor, laugh at his jokes, chide him for chasing a cat. He truly didn't mind what she did, he just did not want this moment to end.

"Do not tell my family. Please, please do not tell my family about this." She drew in a deep breath and the pleading look in her eyes was almost too much to bear. She looked too close to tears, and that was not right. This feisty, silly, funny little thing should never have occasion to cry.

And certainly not if there was something he could do to help it. He picked his hat up from where it had fallen on the ground and held it over his heart. "You have my word."

He was rewarded with a small smile before she disappeared. He heard an old man's voice call out to her that her carriage would be ready soon and he...

He had no desire to go inside.

But he had questions, and as the young Miss Purchase did not seem inclined to answer them...

He'd be forced to deal with her family.

## 5

Unlike Miss Louisa, the rest of the family seemed quite happy to see him.

Too happy, as it were.

"Where did you disappear to?" Gregory asked as a talkative Lady Torrent led the way to the drawing room.

"Nowhere."

"Did I hear you talking to someone?"

"No." He could feel Gregory's look of disbelief. "Just a cat."

"A *cat?*"

The hushed conversation was mercifully cut short as Lord Torrent gestured for them to take a seat beside the elder sister, a Miss... Oh drat, what was her name?

"I am certain you remember my eldest daughter, Miss Margaret Purchase."

"Of course," he said with a little bow as he reached the settee where she was artfully posed.

*Posed* seemed to be the best word for it as she did not seem entirely comfortable, but rather, situated in a way to show her best features in the candlelight. Sitting there with that stiff smile, she reminded him of a piece of art...or perhaps a collectible doll like one might buy for a young girl.

"Lovely to see you again, Miss Purchase," he said with as much enthusiasm as he could muster.

Her response was quiet and forgettable, but she seemed nice enough and it was clear that her parents were hoping for some sort of interaction between them when Lady Torrent's stilted conversation became that much more stilted for their attempts to draw Margaret into the conversation.

"Oh yes, the Murphys always did enjoy grand affairs," Lady Torrent said with a forced laugh when the topic turned to shared acquaintances in the countryside where they owned neighboring estates. "Is that not right, Margaret?"

Lady Torrent looked to Margaret with brows arched in expectation.

Poor Margaret's eyes flashed with panic. "Yes," she said quickly. And then when she realized that her mother wanted her to elaborate, she added, "Quite right."

Lady Torrent turned a broad beaming smile his way as if to say, *See? There you have it. Margaret has spoken.*

It was a lucky thing he'd brought Gregory along or the entire night might have been a lesson in cruel and unusual punishment for him, Margaret, her mother—whose cheeks had to be in pain by now with all that forced smiling—and her father, who sat there silently, looking far too serious by far.

Once Gregory discovered that Margaret shared his love of music, he stepped in handily, steering her into a conversation and drawing her out.

Lawrence had known she was beautiful—everyone kept telling him so, after all—but it wasn't until he saw her light up with honest enthusiasm during her conversation with Gregory that he actually believed it.

She *was* awfully pretty, he supposed. If one was partial to thin, tall blondes with perfect features and a mild, composed demeanor.

Gregory certainly seemed to take a liking to the girl.

For Lawrence's part, all he could muster was a pleasant but tepid admiration for her. He wished he felt more, to be honest. He needed to wed to produce an heir, her father owned a neighboring estate, she came from good families. She'd be a solid match.

He found himself musing over this halfheartedly, as he tried to keep his attention on Margaret and her mother, or at the very least on whatever it was Lord Torrent was stewing about in his seat by the fireplace.

Lawrence suspected they were to discuss a sale of property tonight. By all rights, he should be thinking about the logistics that were involved.

He should be thinking about all of these things, but instead, his thoughts kept coming back to Louisa.

It was only natural, he supposed. It was not every day one was accosted by a young lady falling out of a window. And the ensuing conversation had been so odd, so out of the norm, so...charming.

No, not charming,

*Enchanting.*

He hadn't even realized that he'd been grinning over the memory until Lady Torrent met his smile with a frozen grimace of her own. His own smirk faded fast as he once more realized where he was...and with whom.

"You have another daughter, do you not?" The question was admittedly abrupt.

The room seemed to freeze. Only Gregory did not tense at the innocuous question. "Why, yes!" Lady Torrent's voice was a little too loud and far too shrill. "That is right, you have met Louisa, have you not?"

"Not properly," he murmured.

Wrong thing to say.

He realized it instantly but he had not been thinking. Poor Lady Torrent looked stricken.

"She seemed a charming young lady," he added quickly, and the older woman's expression eased with relief.

Had she honestly expected him to sit here and berate Louisa for dancing in her night clothes some six months after the fact? He might not be known as the most effusive conversationalist, but he was hardly so callous as all that.

"She is charming," Margaret said quickly. "Very...er, *spirited.*"

He made a noncommittal noise of agreement but Lord Torrent cut short any more talk of Louisa right before he could find a way to suss out why on earth she'd have been escaping her own house via a window.

"Shall we take a moment away from the ladies to discuss the land we're offering to sell?" Lord Torrent finally broke his broody silence and at the most inconvenient time.

Lawrence forced a small smile. "Yes. Certainly."

He followed the older man into his study and sat through yet another round of meaningless chatter before Torrent got to the issue at hand.

The land.

Lawrence had been prepared for this. Obviously. It was the whole reason he was here, he'd never doubted that.

What he was not prepared for was for a certain young lady to be thrown into the bargain.

The *wrong* lady.

He shook off the thought. There was no right lady, only an unwanted proposition. One that he had most definitely not seen coming. He stared at Torrent for a long moment after the man stopped speaking. To his credit, the gentleman did not so much as fidget beneath his stare.

Now he knew where Louisa got her nerve, he supposed.

She had her father's backbone and her mother's green eyes. But where had that blazing red hair come from? It made her look like a flame come to life. Bold and beautiful, and with a mind of its own.

Right. He'd officially lost track of this conversation. "Are you suggesting that..." He cleared his throat as he tried to find the right words. "You would like my marriage to Margaret to be a part of this...sale?"

"No, no." Her father looked offended, and rightly so. "I merely meant... It could be fortuitous for everyone if we were to unite our families." He paused for a moment. "Do you not agree?"

"I, uh..." *Drat.* He should have seen this coming, he supposed. He knew that they were looking to marry off their eldest, and he knew that they were in financial trouble, likely looking to find a wealthy match as well.

He should have seen this coming—he would have seen this coming if he hadn't been distracted by a certain redhead with a penchant for causing chaos in his life whenever she appeared.

Even now...what was he doing thinking about her at a time like this? *Get out of my head, blasted woman.*

To Torrent, he merely inclined his head thoughtfully. "It is certainly worth considering."

This seemed to satisfy the older man and some of the tension left the room.

"For now, however," Lawrence continued. "Let us focus on the sale of the property, shall we?"

"Oh yes, yes," Torrent said briskly. "The sale is quite... That is, the timing of it is quite critical."

Lawrence gave another nod of understanding. Rumor amongst his peers at the club had it that Torrent had gotten up to his eyeballs in debt. Worse yet, he seemed to owe money to some unsavory types. The details had been hazy at best, and gossip best taken with a grain of salt.

However, even the whisper of this sort of gossip was usually rooted in truth.

He had no wish to see the neighboring property of his countryside estate sold off to creditors or stripped apart to make ends meet. And besides, he'd always rather liked the strip of land in question.

Right up until it was time to go into dinner they discussed the details of a deal that he supposed would keep the creditors off the older man's back...for a little while, at least.

By the time they went back to join the others to head in for a meal, Lawrence was not altogether surprised to find Margaret laughing brightly at something Gregory had said. If there was anyone who could put a nervous lady at ease, it was his friend.

Even Lady Torrent seemed to have lost her stiff, anxious edge as she led the way into the dining room with her husband.

He supposed now was as good a time as any to try again, now that everyone was so at ease. He waited until the first course was served before bringing up Louisa in the most nonchalant tone he could muster. "Tell me, where is your other daughter this evening?"

That lovely ease? It disappeared in an instant.

Lady Torrent froze with a spoonful of soup hovering in front of her before she seemed to find her voice. "Louisa?"

He might have imagined it, but he thought he caught Margaret wince at her mother's tone.

Lawrence knew *he* was trying not to wince, so perhaps he was projecting.

"She is at finishing school," Lord Torrent answered on his wife's behalf.

That seemed to calm her because she smiled brightly and

returned to eating. "Yes, we've enrolled her at Lady Charmian's new school for young ladies." Her smile turned beatific. "It is so good for these young ladies to learn the finer points of etiquette, don't you think?"

He managed a smile but it was nearly impossible to keep from making a joke about Louisa's etiquette on the dance floor. Or her charming manners when she happened to land upon a gentleman in an alley.

It was difficult, but he suppressed the urge with a cough and a sip of his wine. His particular brand of humor wasn't entirely welcome at the best of times, and now any attempts to bring levity to the situation would surely go amiss.

Besides, he'd made a promise to Louisa, and so he could not bring himself to mention that he'd seen her not two hours ago. Which still begged the question...why had she been running away? Unless she wasn't running from her family...but from him.

No, that made no sense.

Did it?

He accepted the next course that the servant set before him and took several bites before trying again. "It is unfortunate that she could not join us this evening."

"Mmm." It was difficult to assess whether Lord Torrent's mumbled response was in agreement or disagreement, before he returned to his meal.

Gregory shot Lawrence a questioning look, which he ignored. Not one to sit by idly for long, Gregory turned his attention to Margaret again and the two became engrossed in a conversation about art that Lawrence couldn't quite follow even if he'd wanted to.

He *didn't* want to because he still hoped for an answer of some sort. He'd never had much patience for mysteries and the riddle that was Louisa begged to be solved.

"They must keep your daughter quite busy at this school—"

"The School of Charm," Lady Torrent finished. "Is that not a lovely name?"

"Charming," he joked. His dry tone once again made his attempt at a jest fall flat.

Louisa would have laughed. Or maybe just rolled her eyes with a little huff of amusement.

And since when had he started to predict how that strange creature would behave were she here?

The point was, Louisa was not here, and that was all that interested him—the mystery that was Louisa's bold and graceless escape. "The school must keep her quite busy," he said again, looking around pointedly.

"Oh yes. The girls are always socializing with the best families," Lady Torrent said.

He just barely held back a sigh of exasperation. Right. Enough of this. It was time to be more direct. "I suppose that is why she could not be here this evening?"

No one responded immediately. Finally, Lord Torrent responded stiffly. "I am certain Louisa would have enjoyed meeting you and your friend this evening, my lord, but you know how it is with these young ladies. There is always somewhere they need to be."

"Always on the go!" Lady Torrent added.

*On the go*, that was one word for it. He had a feeling 'sent away' was more apt. Something unpleasant twisted his gut at the thought of her expression just before she'd left. *Do not tell my family you saw me.*

It was starting to become clear now. She was not worried that they'd learn she had been running away, but rather that he had seen her—when clearly he was not supposed to.

The thought did not sit well. Not at all.

Was the girl eccentric? Undoubtedly. But she was also

sweet and vibrant and full of life. She was a breath of fresh air. And right about now, this dining room was feeling claustrophobic with its staleness.

"I am certain you will meet her properly one day soon." Lady Torrent's smile was disconcertingly knowing as her gaze flickered from him to Margaret. "It is kind of you to take such an interest in our family."

He cleared his throat and reached for his wine, not entirely certain how his rather bland remarks about Louisa's whereabouts could have been taken as a signal that he had an interest in their family.

Come to think of it, he wasn't entirely certain what she meant by 'interest in our family.'

It seemed best to back away now, while he still could. Her tone was bordering on...menacing.

Or maybe that was just his imagination.

He caught Gregory smothering a smile as Lady Torrent not-so-casually turned the conversation to an upcoming event at Lord Everley's home to which they had all been invited. Lord Everley was another mutual acquaintance—one who Lawrence knew only slightly but who'd seemed determined that he accept this invite when they'd run into one another at the club.

"I have several invitations for that evening, I'm afraid," Lawrence hedged. "I am not quite certain I will be able to make it."

"Oh, but you must." Lord Torrent had spoken so little throughout the meal that everyone seemed to stop what they were doing to take notice. He dabbed his mouth with a napkin. "I know he's so hoping to better make your acquaintance."

Lawrence held back a sigh. He'd gotten the same impression at the club. He'd also felt a little dirty after their brief run-in. The other man's smile had felt cold, his manners disingenuous, and his eyes held a maliciousness that made his skin crawl.

The fact that Lord Torrent's features seemed to tighten with discomfort at the mention of the man only added to his unease.

"Margaret will be there," Lady Torrent added with an ingratiating smile.

He forced his lips up as well. What on earth was he supposed to say to that? *Oh, well then, I shall drop everything, shirk my commitments and come join you for a tedious soiree.*

"I'm sure Louisa would be happy to join us, as well," Lord Torrent added.

Lady Torrent looked to her husband in obvious alarm before fixing Lawrence with another one of those vapid smiles. "Oh, yes. Certainly. If it is important to you to better acquaint yourself with all members of this family, I am positive that can be arranged."

*I have other plans. Thank you but no. I will have to check my schedule.*

He had several evasive non-answers at the tip of his tongue, and yet what came out of his mouth was, "Then I shall look forward to seeing you all there."

Everyone in the room seemed mightily pleased by this, and he felt compelled to add, "And I will look forward to meeting Miss Louisa under...different circumstances."

"Of course, of course," Lady Torrent said.

He listened with only half an ear as she chattered on blithely about who would be there and what they could expect.

Lawrence didn't care.

He had no use for Everley or his parties...

Unless it meant he'd have another chance to see Louisa.

# 6

*This is it.* Louisa took a deep, steadying breath. The time had come. She was about to have her short life taken from her by her very own mother—and while Miss Grayson and Margaret looked on, no less.

Louisa braced herself for her imminent demise.

"Are you certain that perhaps you are not overreacting?" Addie asked as she pried Reggie from Louisa's embrace. She'd wanted one last snuggle with her favorite little boy before the inevitable.

"Overreacting?" Louisa shot back. "Me?"

Addie's lips were twitching in an obvious attempt not to laugh. "You do not even know for certain if Tumberland mentioned your little...tumble."

"You *tumbled* onto *Tumberland*." Prudence giggled like a child behind her until Louisa shot her a narrowed-eyed glared. Prudence's lips straightened along with her shoulders and the uncharacteristic display of silliness was over.

"Really, Louisa, I don't know how you get yourself into these situations," Delilah said with a shake of her head. Of course Delilah wouldn't understand. She'd been raised to be the perfect young lady and she excelled at it. Oh, certainly, she was more than a little spoiled and her priorities were not altogether morally aligned—but other than that she was exactly the type of young lady that Louisa's mother had always wanted her to be.

Delilah was perfect. Just like Margaret.

"Maybe he did not tell your parents that you—" Addie started.

"Of course he did," Prudence interrupted, seemingly scandalized at the very notion that Tumberland might have kept Louisa's secret. "My father was friends with Tumberland's family. I have it on good authority that he is an upstanding man of high moral character."

*Upstanding man of high moral character?* Louisa wrinkled her nose at that unpleasant description.

Prudence sniffed. "There's no doubt he would have done the right thing—" She fixed Delilah with an insufferable, know-it-all look. "And told Louisa's parents that she'd been running away."

"I wasn't running away!" Louisa had said this multiple times now and no one seemed to understand.

Delilah's brow drew together. "I still do not understand why you did not just use the front door like any normal person would have done."

Louisa huffed. "Well, of course you would say that now. It's clear I should have done so in h*indsight*, now isn't it?" She paced the length of the room nervously. "But that knowledge does me no good now, does it? If he's told my parents that I've embarrassed them again, they will never forgive me. My mother is coming here to throttle me, I just know it."

Addie handed Reggie over to Prudence and then grasped Louisa by the shoulders. "Be strong, Louisa. Even if your mother is here to thrash you, I am positive you will survive."

Louisa sighed at her friend's attempt at levity. "I suppose

you are right." Whatever her mother had in store for her was nothing worse than what she deserved. Truth be told, her guilty conscience was acutely aware that she deserved whatever she got.

She turned to leave the cozy, warm confines of the sitting room where the girls liked to gather, and headed instead for the far more formal drawing room where they met their visitors.

Granted, Louisa never had visitors before. At least not for her alone. She tugged on the sleeve of her gown nervously, sneaking one last glimpse of her reflection as she went to join her mother and the others.

"Ah, there you are, dear!" her mother said with a wide, beaming smile when she entered.

Louisa froze in the doorway. Something was wrong. Something was *very* wrong. Her mother had never once seemed so very happy to see her. She glanced over at Margaret for some clue as to what was going on but all she got there was a half-hearted smile and a rueful look, as if she too were acknowledging the oddity of their mother's enthusiasm.

"Come in, Louisa," Miss Grayson said. As always, the leader of this school was perfectly turned out—every bit the proper lady. All soft-spoken kindness and maternal warmth. All elegance and well thought-out conversations.

Louisa would bet her life that Miss Grayson had never once fallen out of a window.

She stifled a sigh as she took the seat across from her mother. One day she hoped to grow up to be just like Miss Grayson. However, at the age of nineteen, she had to assume she didn't have that much growing left to do.

This time the sigh escaped, but she did her best to plaster on a smile even as she worriedly waited for her mother to drop the happy routine and pounce on her about her idiocy the other day.

It truly had been stupid of her. To climb out the window was one thing, but to sit there and *converse* with the man? To laugh at his ridiculous jokes and then...oh heavens...she'd basically begged the man for a favor.

She'd gone mad, that was all there was for it. She'd temporarily lost her mind. What other explanation could there be? For a brief moment there, she'd forgotten his respectability. She'd even managed to forget the way he'd sold her out after their last encounter.

All she'd seen was the amusement in his eyes and the dry wit in his voice.

For one crazy moment out of time, she'd forgotten he was intended for Margaret, forgotten that he was a high-and-mighty marquess who'd looked at her with abject disdain.

For a brief moment there, she'd thought of him as...a friend.

An ally, perhaps.

Whatever she'd thought in her addled state, she'd been wrong. Clearly. He was the man Margaret was to marry...just so long as she didn't scare him off first.

"Would you care for some tea, Louisa?" Miss Grayson asked. That was what her mouth said. What her eyes said was, *Dear, are you all right?*

Louisa blinked rapidly as she came back to the present. "Yes, please. That would be lovely." She had to assume that what *her* eyes said was, *Not really, but thank you for asking*.

Her mother was determined to torture her, that much was clear. She spent a solid ten minutes asking questions about Louisa's classes, and social engagements, and the day-to-day activities at the school. If she was attempting to kill Louisa by ratcheting up her anxiety, she could not have done a better job of it.

After a quarter of an hour, Louisa's hands were clutching her teacup so tightly, she very nearly broke the fine china. At last, her mother seemed to run out of questions, and Miss Grayson fell silent as well.

Louisa's mother gave her a bright smile. "You'll be pleased to hear we had the most charming visit with Lord Tumberland the other day."

Louisa was certain her false smile would crack her face in two. "Oh?" she managed.

Here it was.

Her mother had just been too polite to murder her before making small talk. Louisa fought the urge to clench her eyes shut and shout out an excuse—

"He took quite an interest in our Margaret," her mother finished with a sly smile.

Louisa blinked.

Luckily Miss Grayson gave the sort of inconsequential response such a statement required, and Louisa's mother took that as an encouragement to regale them all with an excruciatingly detailed account of Tumberland's visit.

She'd been talking for nearly two minutes straight when Louisa finally managed to completely register the fact that... she did not know. Her mother had no idea that Tumberland had caught her whilst she'd climbed out a window.

Oh, very well, *fallen* out of the window.

A lightness stole over her and she understood now how a prisoner must feel after he'd been granted a reprieve.

*She would live to see another day!*

"Have you had the pleasure of meeting Lord Tumberland, Miss Grayson?" her mother asked. She did not wait for an answer. "He is quite handsome. And so very charming."

Charming? She arched her brows as she considered that. With his stern features and serious tone, he hardly fit the description of charming. Certainly, he had a sense of humor, but only the subtle glint in his eyes gave that away.

She supposed that glint could be considered charming.

But no, even with his dry humor and quick wit, no one would call him *charming*.

Now handsome, on the other hand...

A memory of sandy-colored hair and flashing, intelligent eyes, of well-crafted features befitting a statue...or a portrait of a certain deceased seafaring captain.

"He seemed quite smitten with our Margaret," Louisa's mother added with a smug little smile.

Really?

Huh.

Louisa blinked. Well that was...wonderful.

Wasn't it?

She shook her head. Of course it was.

And she shouldn't be surprised. Of course he was interested in Margaret. Why wouldn't he be?

The more pressing question ought to be...was Margaret besotted with him?

Louisa looked to Margaret with interest, wishing that just once they had that sort of close sibling relationship that allowed one to read the other's mind. That would certainly come in handy just about now.

But all she got was that same small smile from Margaret which didn't really tell her anything at all.

Knowing Margaret, she likely was just as pleased as their mother, just far less effusive with her excitement. After all, this was what she'd wanted. What the whole family needed.

Louisa ought to be giddy with relief that a fruitful match was near and her family's financial stress would be a thing of the past.

She should be happy.

She really, really should.

"Is that not wonderful news, Louisa?" her mother asked, apparently catching up with the fact that the normally talkative Louisa had not spoken in a while.

"Yes!" Louisa said a little too heartily. "Wonderful news."

Miss Grayson cast her a suspicious sidelong look at her feigned enthusiasm—Louisa had never claimed to be much of an actress. And even Margaret gave her a questioning glance. But their mother once again rode roughshod over the conversation, talking at great length about Tumberland and his friend, Mr. Allen.

This time, Louisa was all too happy to listen to her mother, particularly if it meant she could avoid speaking herself. She wasn't quite ready to talk at length about the great boon that was Tumberland's courtship of her sister.

It was a good thing, of that she was certain.

She just wasn't quite able to feel good about it.

The hour was drawing to a close by the time her mother finished regaling them with all the wonderful tidbits she knew about Tumberland and his lineage. If Miss Grayson had not already been well-versed in Debrett's she'd surely received an excellent lesson on one particular title and its legacy this very afternoon.

How lovely for Miss Grayson.

Louisa stifled a yawn, plotting how she could steal a moment alone with her sister to gauge her reaction to all this. Margaret might have always talked about marrying well, but Louisa couldn't help but believe that somewhere deep down beneath all that calm pragmatism lay a romantic heart.

After all, they were sisters. Surely they had at least one thing in common, and it was clearly not demeanor or looks, so it stood to reason that perhaps they shared a bent toward romance.

If so, she absolutely despised the idea of her sister marrying for anything other than love. And Margaret did not love Tumberland, of that Louisa was certain. How?

She just was.

"Mother, we ought to leave soon," Margaret said at last.

"Oh, yes! It seems I lost all track of time." Her mother laughed.

Margaret arched her brows as their mother started to set down her teacup and gather her belongings. "Aren't you forgetting something?"

Her mother's expression was blank.

Margaret cast Louisa a quick, almost apologetic sidelong look. "The reason we came," she prompted her mother.

Louisa tensed, studiously ignoring the burst of hurt that came with knowing that her mother had come for some ulterior motive, and not, in fact, to visit with the daughter who'd been staying in someone else's home for six long months.

She pushed the thought aside quickly, however, and fixed her mother with a politely curious expression.

"Oh, of course! How silly of me," her mother said. Still going about her business, she added, "Louisa, we've all been invited to Lord Everley's in three days' time. We expect you will join us."

It was not a request but a command.

"Actually, Mother..." She shot Miss Grayson a questioning look.

"The girls were supposed to go to the theater that night," she said softly.

"You can go to the theater any night," her mother interrupted. Turning to Louisa, her smile faded fast. "You will go. It means the world to me and your father."

Louisa blinked in surprise. "My being there means that much to you?"

"Of course!" Her mother sighed. "Lord Tumberland asked for you to be there specifically. We would not wish to disappoint him, now would we?"

Louisa's heart lurched in her throat. Tumberland had asked for her? *Oh no.* She'd been too quick to believe herself safe. Lord Tumberland had something else planned. Possibly a fate worse than death.

She rolled her eyes when her mother's back was turned. It was very possible she had gone a bit overboard with the drama as of late.

Perhaps Addie was right. Perhaps it was time to read something other than her favorite gothic novels; they were starting to go to her head.

But even so... His requesting her presence—it made no sense. Louisa looked from her mother to Margaret, but neither seemed to sense her distress. What was she missing? "Why would he wish to see *me*?"

Her mother sighed. "Is it not obvious? He clearly wishes to scrutinize Margaret's family before making any sort of promise." Her mother shot a quick look at Miss Grayson before arching her brows meaningfully at Louisa. "Lord Tumberland would not be the respected gentleman he is today if he did not take every measure to ensure his acquaintances were from good families."

Louisa bit the inside of her cheek. *Good families*. Meaning, ones without odd little sisters with a tendency toward melodrama and scandal, she supposed. "Yes, Mother."

But her mother was not done. Moving to stand closer, she lowered her voice. "Lord Tumberland is clearly giving us a second chance to prove that we have raised our daughters to be the epitome of grace and decorum."

Louisa winced as she recalled falling, a tangle of limbs and grunting as she accidentally tackled her sister's beau.

"Your sister has proven herself to be a paragon of virtue," her mother continued.

Louisa felt the blow of the comparison even as she fought the urge not to laugh. *Paragon of virtue*? She snuck a glance over at Margaret and the urge to laugh died quickly.

Oh drat, Margaret *was* a paragon of virtue. While Louisa was only ever a disgrace.

Her mother tilted her head down and gave her a warning look. "Tumberland insists on you being there, so you *will* be there."

Louisa nodded, afraid to open her mouth lest the truth come tumbling out. Her mother had it all wrong. Tumberland was not trying to ascertain whether she had mended her ways...

He was hoping to out her as a scandal.

The thought stung like a betrayal. She had a vision of amused eyes, of a calm, even tone—laughing at her, perhaps, but not unkindly. In fact, for a second there, she'd almost thought he'd been an ally, of sorts. A compatriot in her silly plan to flee the scene.

She stifled a sigh as she realized that she'd been wrong. Again. He might have been laughing, but he'd also been judging. And now he hoped to catch her out once and for all as the disgraceful failure of a young lady.

What other explanation could there be for him to insist upon her presence?

Her mother smiled for Miss Grayson's sake but kept her voice low. "You will be on your best behavior, Louisa. Do you understand?'"

"Yes, Mother."

"Just this once, we will get through a public outing without you causing any sort of embarrassment for your sister."

It was not a question and even if it were, Louisa's throat ached too much to answer. Instead, she nodded once more. It was on the tip of her tongue to protest. To explain to her mother that she never *intended* to cause trouble It was not as though she were a willful, disobedient child, just...curious.

And perhaps a bit too whimsical. But she'd never meant to cause harm.

That had to count for something, didn't it?

Her mother turned to say her goodbyes to Miss Grayson but her smile was still strained.

With a heavy heart, Louisa realized that perhaps it did not matter whether her foibles had been intentional or not. Either way, they'd caused pain to her parents and her sister.

If she were the one who kept her family from finding the financial salvation they so desperately needed, she would never forgive herself.

They all deserved better from her, and there was no more room for excuses. Straightening her spine, she tilted her chin up with resolve, ignoring Margaret's questioning look.

Her sister would see soon enough that this was the start of a new era. Gone was the former childish Louisa with her romantic notions and her quest for adventure. This new Louisa would be all that was demure. She'd be the very picture of docile and well-behaved.

A voice deep in the back of her brain snorted in disbelief. Quite possibly because she'd given herself this speech before. It sounded very familiar and less believable this time than last.

But she would not doubt herself. Not on this.

She would begin her campaign to prove herself at this soiree she was to attend.

It would be the first step in a long road to redemption.

*One night*, she told herself as her mother and sister walked out the front door and back out of her life. *Surely she could stay out of trouble for just one night.*

## ❧ 7 ❧

"I still do not understand why he specifically requested that you attend," Delilah said as the girls watched her get ready.

"You are just jealous that a marquess did not request the pleasure of *your* company at an intimate soiree," Prudence said to her friend.

Delilah merely shrugged, not attempting to deny it. The girl was one year younger than the others but it often seemed that her ambitions to marry and to marry well were greater than all three of them combined.

With lips pursed as she was wont to do, Prudence eyed Louisa warily. "Are you quite certain this is wise? Perhaps you should cry off." Her eyes brightened. "We could tell your mother you have fallen ill."

Louisa frowned at Prudence in the reflection of the mirror. She was nervous enough as it was. "I wish you would have *some* faith in me, Pru."

Prudence had the good grace to wince with regret as she murmured an apology. She did not attempt to say that she had not meant it, however. There was a distinctive lack of 'oh

I did not mean you were certain to make a fool of yourself!' in the silence that followed her apology.

Louisa huffed as she fiddled with her necklace. What were the odds she could get through this evening without sticking her foot in her mouth, at the very least, if even her closest friends did not believe in her?

She turned her gaze to Addie who'd been sitting on Louisa's bed quietly throughout all of this. Too quietly, as a matter of fact.

"What do *you* think, Addie?"

Addie's brows shot up in surprise as she toyed with the duvet. Louisa turned to face her fully now, noticing for the first time just how distracted and distressed her friend seemed to be.

"Addie? Are you all right?"

Delilah answered when she did not. "Addie has been acting oddly all day today."

Now all three of them were facing Addie and Louisa felt a jolt of guilt that she'd put her friend on the spot.

Addie shifted uncomfortably. "It is just that..." She cleared her throat awkwardly and addressed Louisa. "Did you say you were going to Lord Everley's home?"

"Yes, why?" she asked. "Do you know him?"

She licked her lips and glanced around nervously. "In a way..."

Delilah sighed loudly with exasperation. "Really, Addie, we expect melodrama from Louisa, but not *you*."

Louisa shot Delilah a dirty look. "Really, Dee?" She flung a hand in Addie's direction. "She's the one who ran away from an evil villain and very nearly got herself kidnapped...or worse."

Delilah ignored her and Prudence tsked annoyingly. "It's hardly ladylike for you to remind her of that difficult time."

"*Actually*," Addie interrupted. "That's what I was hoping to talk to you about."

All three of them whipped their heads around to face her. It was widely understood that Addie didn't care to dwell on those dark days, and the topic was studiously avoided.

Addie plucked at the duvet again. "Lord Everley..."

"What about him?" Prudence asked with impatience.

"Do you recall when I said I'd overheard a gentleman speaking to Duncan just before I left home?" she asked.

"The one who all but told him to murder Reggie?" Louisa asked loudly. "*Of course* we remember."

Addie bit her lip before blurting out, "That was Lord Everley."

Delilah and Prudence stared in open-mouthed shock but it was Louisa who said it. "Lord Everley is *Lord Evil*?"

Addie winced. That was the nickname they'd given him because Addie had refused to name the man for two reasons. First, her beau Tolston was still quietly investigating the matter, and also—the man had sounded cruel but had not actually done anything wrong.

Tolston and Addie had decided that, until they knew for certain that he had done harm, they could not make any accusations against the gentleman in question.

But now...

Well, now it seemed as though Louisa and her family were entering the den of the devil. Louisa shot out of her seat. "I must warn my father."

"And tell him what?" Delilah responded, her tone irritatingly mild and more than a little condescending in the face of Louisa's outburst. "That Lord Everley was a friend of Duncan's?" She arched her brows delicately. "Half the *ton* was fond of Addie's horrible cousin. No one knew that he was a monster. At least, not until..." She waved a hand in Addie's direction meaningfully.

Addie sighed. "Precisely. Lord Everley never actually did anything wrong."

Prudence looked pale. "But he said those awful things. He suggested Duncan kill your brother."

"He might have been in jest," Delilah said. As if people joked about murder every day of the week.

Louisa wrinkled her nose at the dark-haired princess. Maybe in Delilah's hoity-toity world they *did*.

Delilah shot her a sidelong look along with a scowl. "Oh, stop looking at me like that."

"Like what?" Louisa shot back. "Like you're a monster?"

Prudence snickered. The oh-so-prissy goody-two-shoes had a wicked sense of humor if you took her by surprise, Louisa had discovered.

Delilah? Not so much. She looked down her nose at Louisa. "I resent that."

Now Addie was smothering a laugh and Louisa grinned. "All right, fine. You are not a monster. But admit it..." She planted her hands on her hips. "You would defend the devil himself if he were a wealthy, titled gentleman in need of a wife."

Now they were all laughing, even a grudging Delilah as she rolled her eyes. "You are ridiculous."

"Perhaps," Louisa agreed lightly. "But that doesn't change the fact that I am about to attend a dinner party with an evil villain."

Addie winced. "This is why I wasn't certain I should tell you."

"Are you joking?" Louisa said. "Of course you ought to tell me. I need to be prepared lest this man try to work his evil wiles on me or my sister."

Prudence groaned. "That is precisely what Addie means, Louisa."

Louisa looked to Addie, who gave her a rueful little smile.

"Precisely." Addie's smile softened her words, but only slightly. "I know how important this evening is to you and your family, and I don't want you to do or say anything that might—"

"I would never!" Louisa interrupted.

All four of them took a moment to absorb that lie and Louisa sighed. "Oh all right, fine. I might."

Addie smiled kindly. "Please don't." Before Louisa could interrupt again, Addie added meaningfully, "For the sake of Tolston's investigation."

Louisa shut her mouth, her protest forgotten as she thought about that. "I would not want to interfere in that."

"No, of course you wouldn't," Addie said. "And besides, as of now, we have no proof that he did anything wrong."

"He might just have an odd sense of humor," Delilah added.

They all shot her a look. All anyone truly knew about Lord Everley—aside from this new tidbit—was that he was wealthy as Midas.

And Midas was Delilah's one true love.

Louisa turned to Addie with a narrowed gaze. "Tell me honestly, Addie. What do *you* think of this man?"

Addie stopped fidgeting, her eyes growing wide as she seemed to mull that over. "I would not trust him," she said softly, firmly. "Not for one heartbeat and not with anyone I cared about."

Silence followed that quiet pronouncement.

*And they call* me *melodramatic.* Louisa bit her lip, stopping herself just in time from ruining the solemn moment with that remark.

Instead, she reminded herself of her vow for this evening. She would do nothing improper, nothing to call attention to herself, and nothing to bring her family embarrassment.

Granted, this new information changed things slightly.

But only slightly.

She'd be on alert, would keep her eyes wide open in the event that she saw or heard something that could help Tolston with his investigation. But she'd do it subtly. She'd be like a spy, hiding in plain sight under the guise of the perfect, demure, polished debutante.

"What do you suppose she's plotting now?" Prudence murmured this to Delilah but Louisa heard her.

With a start she realized her three friends were regarding her warily.

"What is it?" she asked defensively.

Addie cringed a bit. "It's just...you get this look on your face sometimes..."

"It almost always spells trouble," Delilah finished bluntly.

Prudence came over to Louisa wearing her most patronizing look of condescension. "Whatever it is you are thinking right now, Louisa, please—" She reached out and gripped Louisa's hands. "Please stop."

Louisa rolled her eyes. "You all exaggerate far more than I ever do. You are aware of this, no?"

They ignored her.

"Please, Louisa," Addie said. "Promise me you won't call attention to yourself with Everley. And please do not get yourself into any trouble because of what I've said."

Louisa went over to her friend and wrapped her arms around her in a tight embrace. "I thank you for sharing this with me, Addie. I know how you are trying to move on from all that awfulness."

Addie hugged her back just as tightly. "Just take care of yourself, please."

"Of course I will," Louisa said. And she'd make sure her parents and Margaret were safe, as well.

And her friends.

She was heading into evil's lair and she would protect everyone she loved from harm.

"Promise me," Addie said again.

Louisa patted her back before moving back to the vanity to finish getting ready.

Delilah's voice was dry behind her as she addressed the other two. "Did anyone else notice that Louisa never actually agreed to that promise?"

# 8

Lord Everley stood beside Lawrence in the townhome's sprawling drawing room where a large majority of the crowd was gathered, talking loudly over one another. "I do hope we can find a moment alone this evening," the host said, his patrician features creasing in a smile.

Lawrence tipped his head. "Of course."

"I've discovered we may have some common interests," Everley added—rather cryptically, Lawrence thought. But before he could explain just what they might have in common, Everley's attention was caught by a society matron, who was waving him over.

"Pardon me," he said. "I must see to my duties."

Lawrence was oddly relieved to see him go. Something loosened inside him as his host walked away, and he could not explain why. To date, his interactions with the older man had been nothing but polite. Boring, even. Discussions about the weather, for the most part. Through it all, Everley had been proper and benign, his voice well-modulated, his posture upright, and his demeanor placid. He was everything a gentleman ought to be, Lawrence supposed.

So why was it the man set his teeth on edge?

He looked around and caught Gregory doing the same, scanning the crowd.

Gregory grinned and lifted his glass in a sort of salute and Lawrence did the same before they both shot a look toward the drawing room entrance.

Irritation shot through Lawrence. Where were they?

Where was *she*?

"Have they decided not to come?" Gregory asked.

"Have you ever thought about pursuing a career in espionage?" Lawrence asked mildly, not turning to look at his friend who'd managed to cross the room and join his side without him noticing. "You move with remarkable stealth."

His friend chuckled beside him. "And you evade questions with similar ease. Perhaps we have missed our calling by not joining the Army."

Lawrence shot his friend a sidelong smirk. "Yes, I am certain they are heartbroken at not having two pampered gentlemen in their midst."

Gregory scoffed. "Speak for yourself, *my lord.* You might be a marquess but I'm a second son. I could do worse than the military."

Lawrence shot his friend a questioning look. "Are you serious?"

Gregory shrugged as he sipped his drink. "I have been giving it some thought," he answered vaguely. "Recently the thought of having something more to offer..." He shrugged again. "Some purpose and a good living..."

Lawrence eyed his friend for a long moment, uncertain of what to say. Gregory was cousin to an earl and came from a family with a vast fortune. More than enough to set him up with whatever sort of life he desired.

Lawrence had always assumed he wanted to live comfortably in London. He knew his friend was expected to make a good match, but beyond that...

Well, he supposed he hadn't given it much thought beyond that.

The notion shouldn't have shocked him as much as it did. He and Gregory had always been on the same page when it came to doing their duties. Neither had ever tried to resist the obligations that were placed upon them. But, at the same time, neither had set out to find some sort of...purpose.

He supposed being a marquess *was* his purpose. The duties involved were time consuming and the responsibilities of his title weighed heavily.

But for a second there he'd felt a pang of...jealousy. He supposed there was no other word for it. His friend was talking about choosing his purpose.

Choosing his destiny.

And the thought left him feeling oddly desolate and alone.

He found himself staring at the doorway once more, no longer even attempting to hide his fascination with the comings and goings at the doorway as more and more people filed in.

He heard music coming from another room and supposed this party was about to get even more crowded and jovial as the spirits flowed and the dancing got underway.

Oddly enough, his own spirits seemed to be sinking quickly and he watched the doorway like a drowning man eyeing the horizon for his rescue.

*There.* At last. He was only dimly aware of Lord and Lady Torrent's arrival, or that of their eldest daughter. His gaze caught by the redhead who hovered just behind them, vibrant in a green gown. She shifted behind her parents, as if trying to hide, but how anyone could miss her was beyond him.

Why would she even try?

The girl wasn't just beautiful, though she had a pretty face and a stunning smile. She was something else. *Pretty* and *beautiful* did not quite cover the certain magic she possessed that made the room seem to come alive when she entered.

For the first time all night, Lawrence took a deep breath.

He could *breathe.*

The stodgy, formal, and familiar atmosphere that surrounded him seemed to brighten until the candlelight dazzled his eyes.

And all because this little imp had arrived.

*Fascinating.*

His lips fought the urge to grin at the mere sight of her, and not only because he was imagining the sight of her white undergarments as she toppled through a window. No, that and the image of her dancing alone in the dark were just a part of it.

The other part of his unexpected and utterly uncharacteristic joyfulness was this wonderful sensation of anticipation.

*What will Louisa do next?*

She appeared the picture of propriety from across the room, but he watched her closely, waiting for her true nature to come bubbling to the surface. He might not have known her long, but he knew only a fool would try to predict what Louisa might say or do next.

How many people were unpredictable?

Lawrence could not think of a single soul who fit that description off the top of his head aside from this impulsive little minx.

He also couldn't think of anyone else who held such a natural, undeniable *glow*. It begged the question—could a person illuminate from the inside out?

His logical brain said no.

But his logical brain was also at a loss to explain the very real, very physical effect she seemed to have on the atmosphere around her. He'd mistaken it for childish delight when he'd spotted her that first night, and then as an air of mischief in the alley, but here, now...

It was clear that she possessed a special magic that was all her own. A *joie de vivre* mixed with curiosity and spiced with kindness.

Whatever it was, it was hers and hers alone.

She smiled prettily at a partygoer who'd joined her and her family. A gentleman whose name eluded him.

Jealousy shot through him.

It was jealousy, pure and simple, no matter how much he told himself that the feeling was not welcome here.

This possessiveness was inappropriate in the extreme. She was not *his* to possess.

*But I want her to be.*

The thought struck him like a gong and left him rattling in its wake.

"Are you all right, Tumberland?" Gregory asked from beside him. "You look as though you have seen a ghost."

Lawrence blinked, and then he let out a choked laugh at the aptness of that comment. How very fitting indeed. She'd mistaken him for a ghost, and he looked upon her as though he'd seen one. It was nearly poetic.

"Did I say something amusing?" Gregory asked, his own brows arched with amusement as he regarded him.

"Not really." Lawrence shook his head, still befuddled by his latest realization. "I think, perhaps, I am suffering some sort of nervous breakdown. Is such a thing possible?"

Gregory laughed beside him, but the sound seemed to lack his normal level of glee. "Well, I have heard that falling for a lady can take a toll on one's sanity. Tolston assures me that once gone, it never returns."

Lawrence's gaze shot over to Gregory, who was looking between him and the viscount's family.

"Falling for..." He started to protest but gave it up quickly. He didn't have the energy to argue, not now when his world had just shifted on its axis at the realization that he wasn't just curious about Louisa.

He was intrigued.

No, that word was still not quite strong enough.

Afflicted, maybe. Or perhaps he was...smitten.

What an awful word for it, but it was far more fitting, though *smote* would perhaps be even more apt. He might as well have been smote by one of Zeus's thunderbolts as he watched Louisa walk into the room with that brilliant smile.

His fingers itched to touch that flaming hair that was currently piled upon her head in some extravagant updo. The curls that had already escaped seemed to be begging him to set the rest of her locks free.

That hair deserved to be wild and free, just like her. Instead, she looked like a tiger in chains as she followed her mother and sister's lead, dipping her head with a demureness that did not suit her as she exchanged pleasantries, that warm smile freezing in place as she no doubt said and did all that was prim and proper.

"I cannot fault you for your judgment," Gregory said. "She is certainly a beauty."

Lawrence murmured some sort of agreement, not entirely pleased to have anyone else noticing her beauty at this particular moment. For some bizarre reason he had this notion that it was for him and him alone. Her odd behavior, her sense of humor, those freckles that teased him, and that hair which was mercilessly restrained...

He had this deep down primal need to possess it. All of it. All of *her*.

She *was* meant for him, of that he was certain.

He glanced over at Gregory, and just like that he stopped fretting over his lack of purpose and choice.

The military might give his friend the sort of direction and freedom he craved, but for Lawrence...

He smiled over at the viscount's family, willing her to look his way.

Lawrence was certain that Louisa embodied the freedom and the purpose he craved. He wanted to look after her, to keep her out of trouble while ensuring that no one dampened her spirit or muted her brilliance.

And *that*, he decided right then and there...

That was precisely what he would do.

# 9

Louisa felt Tumberland's eyes on her from across the room. The pull of his gaze was like a magnet that she was desperate to resist.

*Do not look his way. Do not look his way.*

She had to say it repeatedly to keep her mind on task.

"Do you *see?*" her mother hissed beside her. "Lord Tumberland is looking this way."

Louisa bit the inside of her cheek to hold back a scream. The tension inside of her was ratcheting up, needing a release. If she were a kettle, her whistle would be shrieking to high heaven.

*Of course* she was aware of Lord Tumberland's gaze. She had been from the moment they'd stepped foot inside this opulent home with its overbearing décor. She'd been aware of little else but Tumberland's keen eyes that seemed to follow her every move—judging, and no doubt finding her wanting.

But still, she'd been doing her best to please. To fit the ideal that her mother so desperately wished her to meet. For one night, she could do it. It was just one night.

*Smile, say nothing out of the ordinary, and for heaven's sake—stay out of trouble.*

Easier said than done when the first person to greet them had been none other than Lord Everley himself.

*Lord Evil*, as she had started to refer to him in her head.

Delilah might have been able to come up with excuses for the man, but what sort of person even *joked* about murdering a child?

Only someone truly evil, obviously.

And she was here. In his house. Smiling like a simpleton.

Margaret shifted beside her to look. "I did not see Tumberland," she said as she craned her neck for a view of the gentleman they were all so desperate to impress tonight.

"No, do not look," their mother said through a smile and gritted teeth. "Margaret, do remember to smile. He must see how pleasant you are."

"If he had not yet caught on to the fact that Margaret is pleasant by now, we might want to see if he needs his vision checked," Louisa said.

It was the wrong thing so say. Her mother shot her an exasperated look.

"Sorry," she mumbled. To Margaret she added, "It is just that I imagine you are always smiling around him. You are so very good at that. Don't your cheeks ever hurt?"

"Louisa," her mother hissed before turning to greet a countess.

"All the time," Margaret murmured under her breath.

Louisa nodded. She could believe it. She typically thought of herself as a jovial sort, but this nonstop smiling, even while talking, even when sipping on a lemonade...

It was torture.

Likely because it wasn't genuine. Her cheeks strained against it. Maybe she could slip away to a less crowded room to frown. Just for a little while...

"Here he comes!" her mother whispered urgently in her ear. "Remember, do not speak unless he addresses you, and for heaven's sake, try not to embarrass your sister."

Louisa pressed her lips together and nodded, afraid that if she were to speak she might do something inexcusable...like cry.

She knew her mother had good intentions. They all did. Even Louisa. This night was not about any one person's pride or hurt feelings, it was about the greater good of the family.

And Tumberland?

For better or for worse, he seemed to be their greater good.

"Good evening, Lady Torrent," Tumberland said as he reached their side. He gave a low bow to Louisa's mother and then Margaret before turning to her. "I am pleased you could join us this evening, Miss Louisa."

She managed to maintain a smile even though her insides had gone for a ride. They tumbled about like they used to do when she'd do somersaults in the park as a child. But it seemed they'd gone ahead without her this time, so here she stood—her exterior placid as a rock as her insides frolicked.

It was an effort to maintain eye contact. Why was he looking at her like that? Like she was some specimen to be examined? It was disconcerting.

But, of course, she knew why. He was trying to find fault, no doubt. She clasped her hands together to keep from fidgeting. He would find none, she reminded herself. Delilah, Prudence, Addie, and Miss Grayson had all given her their approval before she'd left, and even her mother hadn't been able to find fault when she'd joined them in the family carriage.

She told herself this, but it did not help this feeling of being *seen*—not just studied or watched, but truly seen. Like he was looking beyond her smile, past the elaborate hairstyle that made her temples ache, and straight through the fashionable gown.

This man was quite obviously examining her, and his expression was unreadable.

*Do I pass muster?* she wanted to snap.

She wanted to, but she did not.

See? Self-control was well within her reach.

"Might I have the honor of your first dance?" he asked, his voice that low murmur she was starting to become familiar with.

She waited for Tumberland to finally turn away to face the lady to whom he was speaking. Her mother and Margaret stood just to her left and they all seemed to be waiting for him to tear his intense gaze from Louisa's face and offer a smile and a hand to Margaret.

He did not turn away.

The silence grew taut until Louisa's mother elbowed her. "Answer the kind gentleman, Louisa."

Her eyes widened, her mouth fell open...

Self-control abandoned ship.

"Me?" she asked, her voice a little too high if the twitch of his eyebrows was any indication.

He cleared his throat. "Yes. You."

"I mean...I just meant...not Margaret?"

Her mother's stiffness beside her was worse than words. When she risked a peek over, even Margaret had dropped her smile to cringe a bit at Louisa's awkward attempts at language.

Louisa drew in a deep breath, held back a sigh of irritation that Tumberland had put her in this untenable situation, and smiled. "I would be honored."

His lips twitched like they had in the alley. She would have bet money that he was trying not to laugh at her, the lout.

But then again, she would *not* bet because she was a *lady.* A proper one, at that.

And if Tumberland was so insistent on judging her this evening, she would do whatever it took to show him that despite the ghost debacle and the alley incident, she could indeed be a sister-in-law who did not disgrace him.

She placed her hand on his arm and let him lead her toward the adjacent room where dancing was already underway. It was a lively reel and she found her smile growing. *This* she could do.

There were few feet close enough to tread on. Best of all, she was able to spin and laugh and enjoy herself when she danced.

"You are happy," he murmured beside her.

She shot him a sidelong look. "Of course I am. Why shouldn't I be?"

His expression was that same bland one he wore all the time but while his facial features were not overly expressive, there was plenty of emotion to be found in his eyes. "It seemed before as though your smile was a bit...forced."

She winced at the accuracy of that description. *Drat.* She'd been trying so hard and she still hadn't pulled it off. "I, uh...it is just that I am not used to such crowds."

"Mmm." His murmur of acknowledgement was tinged with disbelief that she opted to ignore.

"You look beautiful this evening," he said.

She peered up at him with suspicion. Was this another test of some sort? "Thank you, my lord," she murmured when his gaze met hers evenly.

The music came to an end just as they reached the edges of the crowd around the dancers. Before she could even acknowledge her disappointment that they had missed this set, a whole new fear crept in as the music started up again.

*A waltz.*

"Is everything all right?" Tumberland asked.

Blasted man with his keen observational skills.

"Of course." She looked up at him a bit too wide-eyed, perhaps, but she was pleased to note that at least her smile hadn't faltered. "Why do you ask?"

His lips twitched with mirth. "Because you look as though your mouth has frozen in a grimace."

Her smile faded fast with her sigh. Wonderful. They had not even reached the dance floor and she'd failed her first test.

"Do you not enjoy waltzing?" he asked.

She winced as a memory flashed in her mind. Alone. In a nightgown. Dancing with a ghost. She fought back a groan. Would she ever live that down?

Likely not.

"I think I can safely say that I am a better dance partner than...what *was* your imaginary partner's name?" he asked mildly.

If there had been any hint of cruelty in his gaze or his tone, she could not find it. When he looked down at her, she caught the devilish glint in his eyes. He was...

Why, he was *teasing*.

She was torn between irritation and amusement. Laughter won out as it typically did but she bit her lip to hold it back. With a rueful shake of her head she sighed, "Sir Edmond."

"Ah, yes. Sir Edmond." Tumberland gestured for her to lead the way onto the dance floor. "A ghost, was he not?"

Embarrassment washed over her but she always had been good at laughing at herself so the humiliation didn't last long. She tried to keep her mouth shut, but found she couldn't resist taking part in the jest. "I suppose that was a first for you," she teased.

He arched his brows as he wrapped one arm around her

waist and her hand found his shoulder. "Being confused for a spirit, you mean?"

She pressed her lips together.

"Oh no," he said calmly, his voice so mild and so dry it was nearly impossible not to laugh. "I am mistaken for dead men all the time." He frowned. "It's quite insulting, really, now that I think about it." He tilted his head down and she caught that wicked laughter in his eyes. "Am I too pale, do you think?"

"Oh no, not at all." She shook her head quickly. "Although, now that you mention it..." She should not say it. *Do not say it.* "You are rather...*stiff.*"

She said it.

He let out a low, rumbly laugh that had her blinking in surprise. She wasn't certain why, but she'd assumed this man did not laugh. Not really. For all his dry wit, he did not seem the sort to burst out laughing like she was prone to do. He was far too...well, *stiff* for that sort of thing.

Wasn't he?

Memories of their last conversation came back to her. So proper, even when sitting on the ground in the dirt. So serious looking, even when laughing at her.

The man was a riddle. And she always had been keen on riddles.

"Why are you looking at me like that?" he asked.

"Like what?"

"Like you are trying to read my mind."

She smiled at his refreshing bluntness. "Perhaps because I am."

He arched his brows. "And what have you discovered thus far?"

"Pathetically little," she said honestly.

For the life of her she could not figure him out. He seemed so very proper, all wicked glints and subtle humor aside. Her parents and sister certainly seemed to think he was a paragon of virtue and respectability. Even prim, perfect Prudence found him faultless.

But then he said things, he did things...

*He made her feel things.*

She shook off the thought. He was meant for her sister, everyone knew that. Just because he was handsome and had a mischievous glint in his eyes meant nothing. He was only dancing with her as some sort of test, and she'd best not forget it.

"Mmph," he grunted softly as her foot landed on his toes.

"Oh, I am so sorry," she said.

There. See? Her fittingness to be the sister-in-law to a marquess with a long, noble lineage was being tested and she was already failing thanks to her clumsy attempts on the dance floor.

Though she reckoned it was partially his fault for distracting her with talk of ghosts. Perhaps he'd distracted her on purpose, the clever man. She kept her gaze focused on his shoulder as she counted out the steps dutifully, determined not to fail again.

*One, two, three—*

"What are you doing?" he asked.

Her head snapped up as she trod on his toes...again.

This time he didn't so much as wince, and for some reason that made her feel worse. "I am sorry," she mumbled.

"Don't be." The hint of a smile did amazing things to his face. Wonderful things. She'd known he was attractive, of course. No one could deny that. But that little hint of smile softened his hardness and made that wicked glint feel far more friendly.

"I am going to have to assume, however, that while Sir Edmond might have been an excellent companion, he was not the best dancer."

"Indeed, he was not," she said with a sad sigh that made his lips hitch up farther, much to her delight. "Do not misunderstand. Sir Edmond has many admirable traits, but I am afraid that dancing is not one of them."

"What a shame," he murmured.

His eyes danced with laughter and she found it to be infectious. She had to clamp her teeth down on her lower lip to hold back the laugh that bubbled up.

Right alongside the laughter came shock and despair.

What on earth was she *doing*? She was not here for her own amusement—even if the marquess *was* surprisingly amusing.

*Focus.*

But all the focus in the world couldn't keep her feet on the straight and narrow. When she stepped on him for a third time, she whimpered in distress.

Certainly it had been nice for a moment there to be held in his arms—he had surprisingly strong arms—and yes, it had been nice to dance with a partner, for once. But this?

Having him witness what an utter disaster she was when it came to grace and elegance?

This was torture.

He seemed to come to the same conclusion when she trampled on him again.

"Would you care for a breath of fresh air?" he asked mildly.

"Oh, yes please," she breathed. She took his arm and he led the way out onto a balcony that overlooked the gardens.

There were enough partygoers out there with the same idea that it was hardly inappropriate, and yet not so many that she could finally relax. In fact, this new intimacy, being out here alone, for all intents and purposes...it made her that much more on edge.

*Breathe*, she reminded herself. When she inhaled she

caught the scent of lilacs in bloom and...something else. Something far headier and much more potent.

She inhaled again, her eyes closing before they snapped open with a start when she realized what she was doing.

She was *sniffing* him.

Oh heavens. The man truly didn't have to smell so good—like leather, and grass, and something mysteriously masculine that she could not name.

He leaned against the railing beside her. "Better?"

She nodded as she took another deep, calming breath. "Much." Then before she could stop herself, she added, "And I imagine your feet are happy for the relief, no doubt."

He frowned but she caught the hint of amusement there. "A gentleman never discusses his feet in a lady's company." He lowered his voice until it was little more than a growl. "I should hate to shock your delicate sensibilities."

She laughed. "And here I thought I was the one trying to impress you with my proper ways."

His brows arched and the interest in his gaze was unnerving. No one ever looked at her like that—as though her words were fascinating, and not just silly. As though he was eager to hear what she might say next. "Is that what you've been doing? Trying to impress me?"

She shrugged with a rueful smile. "*Trying* being the key word there."

"You do not need to try," he said, so simply, so sincerely, it just about took her breath away. And then his tone shifted and his gaze took on a predatory gleam. "But I am curious, Miss Louisa. Why does my opinion matter to you?"

She stared at him wide-eyed for a moment. Was it not obvious? Her entire family was practically preparing for his wedding to Margaret as they stood here talking. An ugly, unpleasant sensation made swallowing temporarily impossible. Her eyes darted away, off toward the garden as her fingers toyed with some moss on the bannister.

Oh drat, what *was* this awful feeling?

Surely it wasn't...it couldn't be *jealousy*.

"You seem terribly serious all of a sudden," he said beside her, curiosity clear in his tone.

She finally managed to swallow. Perhaps it *was* jealousy—but that was odd. She'd never been the envious type. All her life she'd come second—in her mother's eyes and her father's, in the birth order, in looks, in charm, in skills.

She'd long ago realized she could not compete with her sister so it was easier to not even try. It had worked out well that they had such different interests and tastes because they never seemed to have the same aims, the same goals...they had totally different dreams.

So why now—why *here* of all places—did she suddenly, and quite desperately, want what Margaret had?

She risked a sidelong peek and saw concern written all over his face.

"Louisa," he said softly. "What is it?"

*I think I might want you for myself.* She bit her lip. Of course she could not say such a thing. Just because he was kinder than one might first imagine, and had the sort of odd sense of humor that she now knew she adored, and the sort of handsome features that any girl would drool over...

*Oh drat.* What was she on about? Oh yes. She stared right back into his eyes and reminded herself of where she was and, more importantly, why she was here.

Not to flirt with her sister's beau, that much was clear. She was here to impress him. To prove to him that she was not, in fact, a liability.

The thought was humbling, to say the least.

She shifted away from him. "Thank you for the dance, my lord."

"My lord, hmm?" He leaned forward slightly as if trying to get a glimpse of her face in the shadows. "I rather thought we were beyond the formalities."

She shifted away again, realizing a bit belatedly that she was steering them into the shadows, behind some potted trees. Not quite entirely out of sight of the others, but not in full view either. She muttered an unladylike oath softly to herself, but he caught it.

Of course he did.

"Is there a problem?" he asked.

She shook her head no but he did not seem appeased. She just barely held back a sigh as she admitted the truth. "It is just that...despite my best efforts, I cannot seem to do anything right."

His eyes moved over her, studying her face like he was reading a particularly intriguing passage of his favorite book. "You are too hard on yourself."

She gave an unladylike snort of disbelief and then barely refrained from groaning in irritation over that scoff that gave away too much. At times, it seemed she was her own worst enemy. "I've been trying, my lord," she said again.

"So you've said. Trying," he repeated. "Is that what you've been doing?" He reached out and stunned her stupid when he gently tucked a stray curl behind her ear.

"Y-yes," she managed. "I've been trying so hard to be proper and graceful and...and..."

"Boring?" he offered.

She didn't know whether to laugh or gasp at his comment and what came out was a humiliating mix of the two. A sort of hiccup-giggle that could not possibly be called delicate nor demure.

*Oh, hang it all.*

She decided right then and there that she would never impress him with a perfect demeanor but she *could* appeal to him as a man. He was a gentleman, and a kind one at that, from what she could deduce. After all, he'd only teased her in good humor about the ghost incident, and he had not told her family about her disastrous fall from the window...

Despite what Margaret and her mother might think, he wasn't all that terrifying, nor so very unforgiving. Appealing to his kindness just might work.

"I'm nothing like Margaret, I know that," she started.

"*Thank heavens for that.*" He murmured it softly and she was certain she'd misheard. There was no way he was pleased to find that his almost-fiancée's sister was a lunatic who could not dance.

She swallowed and tried again. "I do not have Margaret's perfect manners, but I do know that I would never intentionally cause any harm to my sister's good name, or that of her... her *family*."

His brows drew together. "Remind me again why we are talking about your sister and her family? Are they not your family, too?"

She pursed her lips in annoyance. Was he being purposefully obtuse? Must she spell it out for him?

By his puzzled look, the answer seemed to be yes.

"Lord Tumberland," she said, straightening to her full height and turning to face him head-on. "I know what you are doing."

"Do you?" he asked, that little lopsided smile teasing her.

"I do," she said. "I know what this is about."

He leaned against the balustrade beside him and tilted his head to the side. "I am certainly happy to hear that one of us does."

She huffed in exasperation. Here she was trying to be noble and forthright, and this impossible man was *laughing* at her.

# 10

It was impossible not to laugh at her.

In the nicest way, of course. It was just that she was so sweet, and so genuine, and so...adorable.

All flustered and frenzied one minute and laughing at herself openly the next.

She was like no one he had ever known before, and that feeling was back. The feeling of finding fresh air after living in a stagnant cave. Of seeing life in all its color for the first time. Of digging in the dirt and coming upon a rare gem, something not of this world.

Her freckles were more prominent against her pale skin out here in the moonlight and he found himself tracing their pattern with his eyes as she sighed heavily, the gesture making her chest rise and fall.

Much better to keep his gaze on her freckles than allow himself to take in the perfectly feminine lines of her body and the lush curves that seemed to thwart society's standards as much as she did.

She muttered something he could not make out, but that was all right. He'd found himself dizzyingly out of sorts throughout this entire conversation. One minute they were talking about ghostly dance partners and now it seemed he was being accused of judging her harshly.

"I promise I will be good from here on out," she said, interrupting his thoughts. "I will be the epitome of a fine young lady."

He tried to imagine this irrepressible imp being quiet and proper. He fought a grin. No, he definitely could not imagine it. She would not be who she was if she wasn't being curious and adventurous and inquisitive and—

"Is this another test?" she demanded. Her hands were clasping and unclasping in front of her in agitation. "I've failed again, haven't I?"

He was horrified to see tension replacing her natural, jubilant happiness. He'd never before met anyone so close to laughter at any given moment, so it was startling to see her so visibly distraught.

He watched as she steeled her features and straightened her shoulders, adopting the sort of posture and expression that screamed 'cool, aloof, and untouchable.'

He hated it. She was hiding away the girl that was driving him mad, and he would not stand for it.

Reaching out gently, he stroked his knuckles over her jaw, watching with delight as her lips parted and her eyes grew dark and dazed.

She felt it too, this dizzying pull, this inexplicably intense attraction.

He was dying to kiss her. Aching to feel her lips against his, to taste her sweetness and revel in her softness. He leaned in slowly, giving her ample time to back away.

She did not.

Her gaze looked mesmerized as she watched him move closer, closer...

When his lips found hers, she sighed softly as if in relief.

Heat coursed through him at the feel of her lips moving against his, shyly meeting his kiss as he grazed his mouth over hers.

He wanted to tug her into his arms and deepen the kiss but the sound of the balcony doors opening behind him had him pulling back instead.

His heart thumped wildly in his chest, and he knew.

He just knew.

Nothing would ever be the same.

Just like he knew when he'd inherited the title or when he'd gone off to school or when he'd lost his parents... This was one of those moments, albeit a good one. A precious one. He met her gaze as she blinked her way back to reality and he knew—his life would never be the same now that he had kissed Miss Louisa Purchase.

"You kissed me!" Her exclamation made him jump slightly and he turned quickly to make sure no one had overheard.

The few partygoers who'd come outside were talking amongst themselves. They'd thankfully been spared an audience, but not out of any gentlemanly consideration on his part. He'd lost his senses entirely and had very nearly ruined this young lady with one maddening, impulsive kiss.

He was nearly as stunned as she was by his actions now that reason was returning.

"Er..." He cleared his throat. "Yes, I did."

Her shout hadn't exactly been one of excitement or happiness. She'd sounded almost...horrified, to be honest.

"Is that all right?" he asked, rather belatedly.

She pressed her gloved hand to her lips, her eyes wide in disbelief. Oh drat, perhaps he'd read this all wrong. He'd been so certain she felt the same...

He'd only meant to tease the real Louisa back to the surface this evening, to draw her out and let her see how much he admired her. He scratched at the back of his head as she scrambled backwards, hissing the words again. "*You kissed me.*"

Perhaps he hadn't quite thought this through.

She was unique, certainly, but she was still a proper, gently bred young lady and she had no way of knowing how serious his intensions were. He cursed himself thoroughly for not taking the proper steps before kissing her.

"Louisa, let me just say—"

"Was this part of the test?" she asked.

"Er..." Confusion had him blinking rapidly. It wasn't the first time she'd mentioned a test, and he still had no clue what she meant. "What test are you speaking of, exactly?"

She rolled her eyes. "I know that you wanted me here tonight so you could ensure that I was good enough to be attached to your family."

"Did I?" His brows shot up because, honestly...what on earth was she talking about?

She nodded quickly, her eyes darting around in panic. He stepped to the side lest she was trying to flee and somehow felt trapped.

But she didn't run. Instead, she reached out and thwacked his shoulder.

Hard.

"Ow," he complained, though not without a good deal of amusement. He could count on one hand the number of times he'd been struck in any way and not one of them had been by a woman.

Though if he counted the number of times she'd accosted his feet on the dance floor, he supposed that number was significantly higher.

"You...you...you *callous* man," she said.

He could practically see how irritated she was with herself at the tame insult. He thought to offer her some better alternatives but she was speaking again, so he thought it best to keep quiet.

"You cannot just kiss a lady like that." She huffed and looked around as if for confirmation. "Even I know that."

He opened his mouth to explain that he *never* kissed ladies like that. No kiss he'd shared with anyone had ever been anything like *that* one. But again, she was too quick.

"What were you hoping to achieve?" she demanded. "My ruin?"

"What?" Now it was his voice that was too loud...but honestly. Why on earth would he wish to ruin the lady he hoped to marry? It made no sense! "No, of course not. Louisa, I think there has been some misunderstanding—"

"Oh really? Do you think so?" She planted her fists on her hips and the sarcasm that dripped from her lips was nearly his undoing.

Blast it all if he didn't want to scoop her up in his arms and marry her right this second so he wouldn't have to face another moment on this planet without this delightful lady at his side.

"Don't you dare laugh at me right now," she growled.

He tried not to. Lord knows he tried.

He failed.

"I'm sorry," he said quickly as a huff of laughter escaped. "My dear, I am truly sorry to laugh, but you must admit. Your response to being kissed is a bit...extreme."

She glared at him. "And how do most ladies react when you kiss them without any warning and when you are supposed to be *courting their sister*?" She held a hand up to stop him from protesting, but he couldn't have if he'd tried.

Her sister?

Was she on about her sister again? His mind whirled with the attempt to keep up. "What does your sister have to do with any of this?"

She blinked once. Twice. Thoroughly stunned, apparently. "Everything." She tilted her head to the side, and now it was she who looked confused.

Well...at least he wasn't the only one flummoxed by this conversation. There was some comfort in that.

"Doesn't she? I mean, Isn't she..." Louisa flailed her hands in a helpless gesture. "Isn't Margaret what this is all about?"

He narrowed his eyes, praying for patience and striving for seriousness so they could sort this out, but really all he wanted to do was toss his head back and crow to the rooftops that he'd finally found his match. The woman of his dreams. The lady of his heart.

He cleared his throat. "Let us start from the beginning, shall we? I asked your family to bring you here tonight because I wanted to see you."

She narrowed her eyes as well, so they were now peering at each other cautiously. He imagined to any bystander they'd look like wary adversaries squaring off.

"That's the only reason?" she finally said.

He opened his mouth to say yes, but stopped. He didn't want to lie to Louisa. Not now, not ever. "No," he said. "Not the only reason."

He hoped she did not push for him to explain because he was at a loss as to how to tell her that he'd wanted to ensure that her parents did not hide her again out of embarrassment or shame.

There was no way to say that without hurting her feelings.

She pinched her lips together with a sigh as she studied him. "No, I thought not. My mother was right. I am here because of Margaret."

He quirked one brow at the resignation in her voice. "I do not think we are talking about the same thing right now."

"My mother warned me that you would be testing me." She sighed, her expression anguished as she jabbed a finger into his chest. "I suppose I've failed, haven't I? Well, I will tell you something, my lord. It is one thing to test a lady, but quite another to...to *tempt* her."

His eyes widened but he wouldn't let her push him away. She'd gotten this all wrong. Or maybe *he* had. Either way, this misunderstanding had gone on long enough. "Wait just a moment, Louisa. I can explain, I promise."

She crossed her arms with a huff, as if daring him to try, his spirited, flaming little angel.

"I honestly do not know what you mean when you accuse me of testing you, and as for *tempting*..." He stopped. His whole body still as the full force of what she'd said struck him in the gut and nearly leveled him at the knees. "You're saying that I tempt you?"

Her gaze widened and her cheeks grew pink as she licked her lips. "Uh...that is...er—" And then she smacked his arm again. "Yes, you beast. You tempted me into kissing you and I revealed just what a foolish girl I really am."

He grinned. He couldn't help it. No one had ever outright called him tempting before. He found that it went to his head. He shifted against the rail, his voice lowering along with his head. "So...I tempt you, do I?"

She scowled. "Do not tease. It is not kind." She gave a haughty tilt of her chin. "I am starting to believe that *you* are not kind. Not to me and definitely not to my sister."

"Right," he said, straightening as he frowned down at her, back to business once more. "Can we please resolve whatever issues you have with your sister, because I have to admit, you are driving me mad every time you mention her."

"That's probably your guilt speaking," she said, her tone nothing less than saucy.

"Guilt? For what?"

"For kissing me instead of her," she said.

He blinked rapidly and finally—*finally*—his sluggish brain

started to keep up. "You think I have a special interest in your sister."

"Of course I do," she fairly shouted back at him. "Your match with my sister is all anyone can talk about."

"Anyone, hmm?" Something rotten started to brew inside him as he realized what she'd thought, what she must be thinking... "Anyone wouldn't happen to be your sister and your parents, now would it?"

His guess was not quite a leap of the imagination. He felt fairly confident that if his so-called impending engagement to a woman he barely knew was the talk of the town, he'd have heard about it by now.

Her confused scowl was the confirmation he needed. Louisa's family had taken his visit to mean more than it did, and his polite inquiries to be something far more.

*Oh dear.*

He ran a hand through his hair, mussing it thoroughly, no doubt. "Louisa, I promise you, I never had any intentions of courting your sister."

She blinked in shock. "You didn't?"

"No."

They stood there for several minutes in tense silence. He was waiting for some sort of reaction—

When she groaned miserably, he shoved his hands into his pockets with a sigh.

That was not the reaction he'd been hoping for.

He watched her fret for another long moment before clearing his throat. "I rather thought that might be viewed as *good* news considering I only kissed you not two minutes ago."

"I know, and that was terrible," she wailed.

He grimaced at the no-doubt unintended insult. "You certainly know how to keep a gentleman's ego in check, I'll give you that."

Her eyes widened at his rueful teasing. "Oh no, I did not mean— I merely meant—" She stopped suddenly and gazed up at him with such earnestness his heart ached. "Are all kisses like that?"

"Like what?" he managed through a dry, croaky throat.

"Like..." She flailed a hand. "Magic."

His heart was officially lost. It was out of his chest and into her hands. He claimed no ownership of the organ as of this moment. "No," he said seriously, trying to match her earnestness. "Definitely not."

She moaned again, clapping a hand over her mouth as she mumbled. "This is terrible."

"*Not* the kiss," he clarified, hoping to make her smile.

It worked, if only briefly. She gave him a small smile as she rolled her eyes in exasperation. "No, not the kiss. Just...*this*." She gestured to him and then to her.

Not much better, really.

"Why, exactly, is this terrible?" he asked.

She sighed like he was a dim-witted school child. "Because everyone is hoping you will marry Margaret."

He studied her in silence for a moment, trying not to be distracted by the way she was worrying her bottom lip. He had questions. Many, many questions. But one seemed to take priority over them all. "Do *you* wish for me to marry Margaret?"

Her head snapped up, and whether she knew it or not, the answer was there in her eyes. Still, he waited her out. He needed her to say it. He needed her to *know* it.

"No," she finally said, her voice soft and sweet. "I do not want you to marry Margaret."

A tension he hadn't even known was there eased out of him so suddenly he was forced to lean against the balustrade once more lest he fall at her feet. "Very well, then."

She frowned. "Very well? Is that all you have to say on the matter?"

He arched his brows, torn between amusement and frustration, because honestly...when had anyone ever spoken to him like this? Only his closest friends, on a rare occasion, but certainly not a young lady he was supposed to be courting.

He *was* courting her, was he not? It seemed that matter was still up for debate.

He scrubbed a hand through his hair in confusion. He wished to court the girl, was that so hard? He'd never known wooing someone could be so difficult. His lips twitched with mirth—then again, he'd never attempted to woo anyone like this girl.

He ought to have known it wouldn't be simple.

"What am I going to tell my mother?" she asked. "And Margaret?"

This last part was said on a horrified whisper that embodied more melodrama than anything he'd ever seen on Drury Lane. "Let me deal with your parents," he said sternly.

It was about time he took control of this situation.

She widened her eyes in disbelief, not at all cowed by his sternness.

He loved that about her.

She planted her hands on her hips. "And Margaret?" she demanded. "Are you going to be the one who breaks my poor sister's heart?"

That shocked him into a stunned silence. "Break her heart?" he repeated in dismay. He looked around the balcony quickly as he tried to remember and analyze the few times he'd been in the same room with her elder sister. "Is she..." He cleared his throat. "Is Margaret very much in love with me?"

Her lips twitched and he caught a glimmer of laughter in

her eyes, before she said seriously, "I do not believe so, my lord."

He sighed with relief and amusement. She was laughing at him, the little minx.

"But the disappointment," she added meaningfully. "She has her heart set on a good match, one that would..." She bit her lip as she trailed off, but he knew what she would have said.

They had their hopes set on Margaret marrying someone who could help save them from their financial difficulties.

The girl was worried about her family. He hadn't thought it possible that he could feel any more for this little imp of a lady, but it seemed he was wrong. A protective instinct he hadn't known he possessed swept over him like a wave.

He tilted his head down, his chest swelling with tenderness. Everything in him cried out for him to reach out to her and pull her close. He wanted to tell her that she need *never* worry. Not for her family, not for anything. Soon enough, perhaps. For now, all he could do was grasp her hands in his and hope that she understood his sincerity.

"It will all be all right, Louisa. Of this I am certain."

She peeked up at him through her lashes and he barely stifled a groan of longing. Big eyes and full lips tipped up toward him and he leaned down, unable to stop himself. "I should very much like to kiss you again."

Her lids started to flutter shut but just before his lips met hers, she pulled back with a gasp. "Wait."

He waited, but it very nearly killed him. Never in his life had he wanted anything more than the feel of her soft lips on his. For a man who'd never fallen victim to the typical vices like gambling and drinking, he was fairly certain this was what it was like to be in one's thrall. The longing, the craving...the heady addiction.

He swallowed thickly as he pulled back. Above all, he was

a gentleman, he reminded himself as he straightened his cravat. But it wasn't the *not* kissing her that stung so badly; it was the rejection. Perhaps this was not as mutual as he'd thought.

"You look ill," she said bluntly.

"Yes, well..." He forced a small smile. "I'd rather thought I was making progress in my attempts to woo you."

"You are!" Her eyes widened as her cheeks stained pink. "That is, you were. It's just that..." She wrinkled up her nose. "I cannot allow you to kiss me again unless I know that Margaret is all right with it. She is my sister," she added with a little plea.

He sighed. Who could argue with that? He tipped his head in agreement and was rewarded with a brilliant smile.

It was dazzling, really. So heady he forgot words altogether and stood there mute, taking her in.

She was lovely. Beautiful and vibrant and brave and—

"Are you certain?" she asked.

He huffed with amusement. "I am many things, Louisa, but fickle is not one of them."

It was the truth. He knew himself, and he trusted his instincts. He trusted his *heart*. And there was no doubt in his mind that his heart wanted this lady, whether or not she drove him crazy.

Maybe *because* she drove him crazy.

She made him feel, and that was worth more than any amount of sanity.

But he did not say all that to her because he had a notion that whatever it was that was causing that doubt to fill her eyes had little to do with him, and everything to do with her.

"What is it, Louisa? Why do you look so afraid?"

She let out a long exhale. "I...I do not know whether to believe you."

His brows shot up. "You question my honor?"

"I question your sanity," she retorted quickly.

He let out a bark of a laugh and watched with something akin to pride as her lips twitched up in return.

"What if this is one of those tests my mother tried to prepare me for?" she asked.

He shook his head. "With all due respect, it is your mother who needs to check her sanity."

"With all due respect?" she repeated. "That is not respectful at all. You cannot just add 'with all due respect' before a statement and expect it to be respectful."

He grinned. "See how much I have to learn from you? I think this will be a mutually beneficial courtship."

Her lips parted. "Courtship," she repeated the word on a breathless sigh, like she was trying out the word for the first time. "But you barely even know me, and what you do know—"

"Is that not the purpose of a courtship?" he asked. "Allowing two people who might be a good match to learn more of one another."

She pressed her lips together, and he took that to be agreement.

"I am afraid you will be disappointed," she blurted out quickly.

"Why on earth would you think that?"

She nibbled on her lower lip, apparently not realizing how badly it made him want to kiss her. "Because I am trouble."

He couldn't help it. Those words coming from that sweet face, so earnest and so honest... "Well, that works out quite well for me. You see, I happen to love trouble."

# 11

*I happen to love trouble.*

The words swirled around Louisa in a happy haze long after Lawrence deposited her with her mother and father. Before he'd walked away he'd muttered a mysterious comment under his breath, for her ears only, about how he would handle matters from here.

*Handle matters.* What did that mean?

Would he speak to her father?

She hoped he would not until after she'd had a chance to break this news to Margaret. But Margaret was nowhere to be found as she stood at her mother's side. Apparently, she'd been whisked onto the dance floor and had been there ever since, and for that Louisa was grateful.

How on earth was she going to tell Margaret that Tumberland was not interested in her?

*That he is, in fact, smitten with me?*

She shook off the thought, because every time she tried to reconcile herself with that element of her tryst—she could not do it. The very thought seemed ludicrous. It had out on the balcony, and now here, beside her parents, watching her beautiful, graceful sister waltz past in all her perfect glory, the thought seemed more unbelievable than ever.

Tumberland wanted her.

Not Margaret, but *her*.

She could hardly believe it.

She stared into the crowd in a daze as her parents talked to an elderly couple beside her. No matter how hard she tried, she could not quite wrap her head around the fact that he had chosen her.

That he'd *kissed* her.

Her lips still stung from the sweet caress, so she knew she hadn't been imagining *that* part, at least. But everything else...?

From the moment he'd walked away, she began to doubt that conversation had even happened. He was teasing; she was dreaming; the entire conversation had been a fantasy... All of those options sounded far more likely than the fact that Tumberland had willingly chosen her above all others.

She narrowed her eyes and pursed her lips as she once again tried to imagine a world in which Tumberland had chosen her over her sister.

Impossible.

It was official. She'd finally gone and lost her mind.

The way he looked at her, the way he spoke to her, the way he kissed her...

It was like something out of a dream. It had been like one of her childish fantasies, but instead of a very lovely, but very invisible, Sir Edmond, the fantasy had featured a living, breathing gentleman.

*A gentleman who'd kissed her.*

"Are you quite all right, Louisa?" her mother asked. "You look terribly pale."

"I am fine," she said quickly.

"How did you get on with Lord Tumberland?" her mother asked.

When Louisa glanced over her mother was peering at her like this was some criminal investigation. Did she know? Did she guess?

"Fine," Louisa said, her voice too high and breathy.

Her mother's brows drew together sharply. "Louisa," she said, her tone low and filled with meaning.

"Yes?" She was all but squeaking now. Her confusing and overwhelming kiss with Tumberland had left her *squeaking* like a mouse.

"You did not do anything untoward, did you?"

Louisa shook her head. "No, Mother."

*I merely kissed a near-stranger on a balcony where anyone might have seen. And, oh yes, the gentleman in question is my sister's suitor.*

She exhaled sharply. Or was he? She wished she'd had just a few moments in silence to make heads or tails of all that had happened. Her mind was still spinning, and she could not tell which way was up or down in this situation.

Her heart was still doing a jig over that kiss and those words—*I happen to love trouble.* But the rest of her—her reason, her logic, every bit of her life experience—it was forming a curdle of fear in her stomach that would not be denied.

That moment had been too good to be true. Of this she was certain. Moments like that only existed in her daydreams and her fantasies. And books. In a romantic novel, something like this she might believe. But in real life?

No one *actually* fell for the less attractive, less proper, less suitable daughter. No one. Not even a gentleman like Tumberland who was so very different from everyone else she'd ever met.

He was a riddle. A perfect gentleman in the public eye,

but when she spoke to him in private he was filled with a humor and a liveliness that no one would suspect.

Maybe he was a kindred spirit of sorts, deep down beneath that perfect exterior.

Maybe.

Or maybe she was a fool for trying to believe in something that was so clearly too good to be true.

Her logical brain was voting for the latter.

"Mother, out of curiosity..." she started slowly.

Her mother's eyes narrowed farther. "Nothing good ever comes of your curiosity, child."

"Yes, well..." Louisa cleared her throat. "Are you certain that Tumberland plans to court Margaret?"

Her mother's look said it all. *You have lost your mind.* "Of course I'm certain. Why would he not? She is the perfect match for him."

"Mmm, quite," she murmured, focusing her attention of the crowd around her rather than on what she ought to say in response to that. *It's just that he kissed me, you see...*

Surely *now* was not the time to tell her mother about what had just happened.

Besides, Tumberland had said that he would handle it.

She tried to calm her nerves but her mother's fidgeting beside her did not help. "Are you certain you did nothing with which he could find fault?" Her mother wrung her hands as she whispered under her breath. "Oh, I should never have left you alone with him. Tell me honestly, did you make a fool of yourself? Did you do anything improper?"

Louisa bit her lip. While she might have stirred up trouble in her lifetime, she'd very rarely lied to anyone, most especially not her mother. "No, mother. But—"

"Thank goodness," her mother said with a sigh. "I've heard things about him."

Louisa blinked. "What things?"

Her mother waved a hand as if it were not important. "Just that he has very high expectations for the young ladies he meets. With everyone, really." She shook her head in what seemed to be admiration. "He is such a good man, so solid and serious. He shall make an excellent husband for Margaret."

"Um," Louisa managed to mumble. It did not matter what she said because her mother was barely paying attention.

"Your father was worried that the little run-in you had with him in the middle of the night would be enough to end things, but I told him that Tumberland had enough good sense to see that Margaret's value more than made up for your...foibles."

Louisa swallowed thickly. *Foibles*. Was that what they were? Her mind flashed on that moment outside. The more seconds that passed by the more she was uncertain whether or not she'd imagined it.

Oh, she knew she'd been alone with him. That he'd kissed her. That the kiss had made her lose her senses as if the world had been spun upside down in a heartbeat.

But everything else—the look in his eyes, the tenderness in his voice, the certainty with which he'd spoken. It was all starting to feel a bit too perfect.

Like a dream.

Like perhaps she'd been so lost in the moment, she'd read the situation all wrong.

Fear had her sucking in a big gulp. She wanted to continue to cling to it all, to revel in that happy haze, but reality was setting in quickly and then as it sank in, the memory of that interlude grew more and more difficult to believe.

Her mother sighed loudly as she pulled out her fan and began waving it furiously. "I must say, I am relieved. With the way he'd singled you out earlier, I'd been sure he was going to try something."

"Try something?" Louisa forced a laugh. "And you accuse *me* of being melodramatic."

"Don't be naïve, dear," her mother said, her tone deadly serious. "Men like Tumberland take their choice of brides very seriously. He would need to be certain that Margaret's family did not have any..."

Louisa braced herself for whatever name came next.

"Black sheep."

*Black sheep*. Louisa pursed her lips. Not the worst name she'd heard for herself. But her mother's words were settling uncomfortably around her, sinking into her skin and seeping into her bones.

The difference between how she'd felt just moments ago and how she felt now was nothing short of monumental.

But of course, *then* she'd been in Tumberland's arms, cloaked in darkness and surrounded by his warmth and his scent...

And now? Now she was alone. On the outskirts of this party, feeling too short, too round, too loud, too gauche, especially beside her mother.

She found herself searching the crowd for Tumberland, as if the sight of him might help to remind her that it had been real.

It *had* been real, had it not?

There! She spotted him on the other side of the room, and her heart did a flip at the sight of him.

He truly was handsome.

Too handsome, perhaps.

She blinked quickly, trying to get a handle on her nerves. He was just as handsome as Sir Edmond, and she'd had a difficult time believing that *he* was falling in love with her.

And Sir Edmond was a ghost.

It was suddenly imperative that she speak to him again. Make certain that what she'd thought she'd seen in his eyes had truly been there. That she had not imagined it all, that the kiss was not some sort of moral test as her mother would likely think if she were to confess what had happened to her mother.

It could not have been all in her imagination...could it? No. Surely not. It was just that she would feel better if he told her so.

Again.

"Will you excuse me, Mother?" she said, already starting to move toward the far side of the room where she'd last seen Tumberland. "I believe I see a friend."

"Fine," her mother said, distracted as she craned her head to keep Margaret in her sights. "But do not get into any trouble."

"Of course not," she said.

Louisa followed the back of Tumberland's head through a long room where partygoers laughed and ate from a spread she hadn't realized had been put out.

Her stomach growled, but she kept going. She nearly lost sight of him when he turned a corner but she caught up and came to a halt when she realized he wasn't alone.

He was following someone else, just as she was following him.

And that someone was Lord Evil himself.

Her breathing grew shallow as she paused in a doorway, her ears strained to make out words but only catching snippets, mainly Lord Evil's low voice.

What could they be meeting about?

Were they friends?

Was Tumberland aware that he was spending time with an evil villain? Her mind's eye called up warm eyes and a sharp laugh that made her want to laugh in turn. Surely, he would not knowingly spend time with a dastardly villain like Lord Evil.

It was her duty to warn him, was it not? She held her breath but let it out as a door down the hallway snapped shut and their voices were cut off entirely.

She entered the hallway and walked past the door slowly. Then she turned and walked past again, even slower this time.

But it was no use.

She couldn't hear a thing. She scowled at the door—the irritatingly thick wooden door that was all but soundproof.

But the windows, on the other hand...

She did not stop to think before moving into action. She'd already come this far, after all. And besides, if she found anything useful, she could tell Addie and Tolston and perhaps her friend could finally get justice for all the badness that had befallen her.

This was what she told herself as she scurried down the hallway and back toward the balcony. No one was out there, which was basically an invitation to slip around the side of the house, into the hedges.

She was definitely not getting into trouble. How could she be when no one was around to spot her?

Her mind raced furiously as she made her way along the brick wall to one dark window and then another. And then she was there. The one lit room and the only open window.

This had to be it.

Sure enough, a low masculine voice filtered through the opening and Louisa drew toward it on tiptoe, trying to make out words.

"You've been awfully cryptic," Tumberland said. "What is it you think we need to discuss?"

"Our common interests, of course."

Louisa shuddered beneath the window. Heavens. That voice! No one had ever fit the title Lord Evil better. Her nickname was remarkably apt if his cold, hard voice were anything to go by.

"Yes, as you mentioned earlier." Tumberland's voice in comparison was warm and low and delicious. An unhurried drawl that refused to waver in the face of evil. "Would you care to elaborate?"

Was it possible to swoon over a mere voice? If so, she was in serious danger. She rested her palms against the brick and went up on tiptoe. If only she could see him, as well. She could just imagine the hard lines of his features in the firelight as he stood up to Lord Evil for all that was good and just and—

"I'm referring to Lord Torrent and his family," Lord Evil said.

Louisa jerked back at the sound of her own name. What on earth did he want to talk about her family for?

"I was not aware you and I shared a common interest there," Tumberland said slowly.

She crept back toward the window. If only she could hear better. If only she could see.

A quick glance around and she'd discovered a log that would put her at the perfect height. As quietly as possible she dragged it over to the window. She'd just put one foot on the edge when Evil's voice stopped her dead in her tracks. "Rumor has it Torrent is in some financial trouble."

Her palms grew moist and clammy inside her gloves as a chill crept over her. Was it so obvious? Did everyone know?

She waited anxiously for Tumberland's response. "Rumor has it, you own his debts, Everley."

Louisa stilled as Everley's cold, humorless laugh floated out of the window over her and gave her limbs a chill she could not shake.

What did that mean that he owned their debts? Why would her father be indebted to this man?

"I simply step in and offer assistance when my friends need my help."

"Your help, eh?" Tumberland muttered something she could not make out. A few more low words were spoken before Everley spoke loudly enough for her to hear again.

"And that is what I called you in here to discuss. I know Torrent is hoping you'll purchase that piece of adjoining land to buy himself a reprieve from the inevitable."

*A reprieve? Reprieve from what? What was inevitable?* The urge to scream just that had her clamping a hand over her mouth as she used her other hand to balance once more on the log. It was covered in moss and her slippers slid a bit before she regained her balance.

Crouching as she was, she could hear better, and would be able to peer in if she were to straighten to her full height.

"Do you have an interest in that land?" Lord Evil continued.

"Of course," Tumberland said evenly, his voice giving away nothing. "It would strengthen my own property."

"Indeed, it would. But at what cost?" Evil said. His tone was wheedling. He was insinuating something, and whatever it was, it made Louisa's blood run cold.

"You need not fear for my fortune, Lord Everley," Tumberland said evenly. "I assure you I can well afford the piece of land."

Evil's voice changed. He dropped any hint of pleasantries as it turned hard as ice. "Torrent means to make his eldest daughter part of the deal."

Louisa stiffened. Margaret. They were talking about Margaret, and Father's hopes that he'd set on her...because he'd tied her to the lands that Tumberland wanted.

"Did he?" Tumberland's voice was so casual, it gave nothing away. Even *she* could not guess if this had come as news to him or if he'd known.

"Don't play coy," Evil said. "I've known Torrent long enough to understand the way he thinks. He's hoping to snare two birds with one stone. Get the money he needs now with the sale of land and financial security from you when you marry his daughter."

Tumberland did not respond.

Not at all.

Louisa was certain she would scream. Why wasn't he saying anything? Why was he not defending her father or denying that he was to marry Margaret?

Why was he so horribly silent?

There was nothing for it. Anxiety and fear and a million other confusing emotions prompted her into action, even though she knew now that this was certainly bordering on trouble.

Eavesdropping was one thing, but outright spying?

Definitely trouble. The promises she'd made to her mother, her father, her friends, and Miss Grayson... Guilt gnawed at her, but she pushed it aside.

This was for the greater good. Why, she might even be able to help Tolston's investigation, and if she managed to suss out more information on her father's plans for Margaret and Tumberland, all the better.

She edged up and up, her fingers scrabbling to keep their purchase and her balance as she peered over the windowsill.

And there they were. Right there. Neither was looking her way, but she could see Tumberland's expression, all stern and serious. No hint of the laughter she'd come to recognize.

Wariness swept over her as she watched this man, so dignified and so regal. So...unfamiliar.

He looked like a stranger, lounging back in his seat with that unreadable, hard expression. He looked...cold. Not like the man on the balcony at all.

That man had been her fantasy come to life, and this man...

This was the man her mother and father and sister were counting on to save them.

"Do you deny it?" Evil asked.

"That there has been some speculation about a match between me and Torrent's daughter? I rarely comment on rumors and gossip, you ought to know that."

Louisa glared at him through the window. That was all he had to say on the matter? Couldn't he have just said *No! I could never imagine a life with Margaret, not when I'm so incredibly besotted with her sister*? Would that be asking for too much?

Evil laughed as if he'd made a joke. "Fair enough."

Tumberland made to move. "If that is all—"

"You have not heard *my* offer yet," Evil said.

Tumberland sank back into his seat, and once more, his expression told her nothing. "Offer?"

"Yes. You see, I recall what it's like to be a young man with the world ahead of him."

Louisa wrinkled her nose at the way he talked. So condescending.

Tumberland turned in her direction and she ducked.

"You are not that much older than me, surely," Tumberland said. "No need to talk as though you are a grandfather."

"Ha!" Evil's laugh held no humor. "I have not even wed yet, myself. But I *am* older, and I remember what it was to be like you."

"Oh yes?" Tumberland's voice was mild but it still made Louisa shiver. There was a hint of danger there she'd never heard in his tone before. It made him sound terribly fierce and magnificently masculine.

If her family and their financial distress weren't currently the topic at hand she might very well have swooned.

"A man like you must hate the idea of being saddled with a wife just to get the property that he deserves."

*Saddled with a wife!* Indignation on Margaret's behalf swept over her. She might not know the particulars, but certainly no one was trying to *saddle* Margaret on anyone. They'd seemed to make a good match, that was all. Defensiveness on her father and her sister's behalf had her justifying the union in her own mind, and that was disconcerting.

She scowled at the brick as she waited for Tumberland's response. *Say something*, she willed. *Say anything. Defend my family!*

The silence that followed was resounding. She gaped up at the window until she could take it no more and then she inched her way up again to see Tumberland leaning forward, his expression thoughtful.

"What exactly do you have in mind?"

Evil chuckled and reached for a snifter. "Ah, I see you're starting to understand."

"It's clear you have some agenda here," Tumberland said evenly. "Why not show your hand so I may return to your party? I'm afraid I've kept some guests waiting for a dance."

"Of course," Evil said mildly. "I wouldn't want to keep you. I just thought you should be aware of a better offer."

"For the land or the girl?"

She hissed in disbelief at the callous way he was talking about her sister, as if she was just another piece of property to buy and sell.

Evil laughed again. "I'm talking about an option in which you get the land without tying yourself to that family, which, let us face it—is certainly only going to drag you down with their debts."

"But they own the land," Tumberland said, accepting the glass of brandy that Evil handed over.

Louisa caught the friendly gesture as she peeked over once more.

"Torrent won't own it for long," Evil said. Even from this angle Louisa could see his smirk. "That land, along with one of his more valuable London properties will be in my hands shortly."

"*If* he cannot make a payment," Tumberland added.

Louisa's mouth went dry and a flash of fear had her scrambling to keep her footing as her feet slid beneath her.

Her father—her poor father. How bad had their situation gotten? How dire were their straits?

She bit her lip as tears stung her eyes but she forced herself to focus.

"Precisely," Evil was saying. "In the very near future I expect to own most of Torrent's properties and his income." He said this as if it were a brag, as if this was something to be proud of. "If you just give it some time—make no commitments one way or the other, I can promise you I will make it worth your while."

"And how is that?"

Evil's laugh held a note of triumph that made Louisa's stomach turn.

"I will give you a far better price for the land, and—" He leaned forward. "There would be no strings attached in terms of a wife."

Louisa tried to swallow but her throat was dry. Tumberland's expression was utterly unreadable and his silence was terrifying.

How could he not be raging against this man? Why would he not be defending her family? Could he not see how manipulative and backhanded Lord Everley was being?

Finally, Tumberland came to stand, and Louisa scrabbled with her hold all over again to keep both men in her sights, ready to duck back down at a moment's notice.

"That is quite the offer, Everley," he said, his voice so smooth and unperturbed, like they'd just been discussing the weather and not her family and their financial downfall.

*Turn back*, she mentally shouted at Tumberland as he headed toward the door. *Do not let him get away with this. Put him in his place.*

"Well?" Evil sounded almost as impatient as she felt as they both watched Tumberland walk away, like he hadn't a care in the world.

"Well, what?"

"Will you consider my offer?" Lord Evil fairly snapped with impatience now. Clearly he was not used to dealing with men who did not cower before him.

And Tumberland most certainly did not cower. She'd be proud of him if she weren't so terribly eager to hear what he might say.

"I'm not certain there is anything to consider, Everley." He stopped and turned and for one terrifying second she thought he looked right at her through the window. But then his gaze was fixed on Everley and she let out a breath. "It seems you have received some faulty information."

"Is that right?" Everley asked, sounding amused. "So you are not interested in the property? Or perhaps you've developed deep feelings for the lovely, insipid Miss Torrent."

Louisa had to fight the urge to leap through the window and slap the man for speaking about Margaret that way and in such a disdainful tone.

"I'd be careful how you speak about the Torrent family, Everley. They are soon to be my family, too."

Louisa's mouth hung open and even Everly seemed stunned for a moment. "Does that mean...you and Margaret?"

"That is exactly what I mean." Tumberland glared at the man as he reached for the door. "Expect to receive payments from Torrent shortly, Everley. Because I have every intention of marrying his daughter."

Margaret. They were talking about Margaret.

He was going to marry Margaret!

Louisa's heart fell into her stomach and for a moment she forgot where she was—just long enough to lose her grip and her balance and to topple backwards with a squeak and an *oof.*

# 12

Lawrence was going to kill her.

First he would kiss her, then he would hold her close, and then he would throttle her.

He'd known she was out there from the start. Or at least, he'd suspected when he heard scurrying outside the window. Luckily, Everley's hearing didn't seem to be as good.

"Did you hear something?" Everley asked now as Louisa's red hair disappeared from view with a squeak.

"No," he said. "But I'd like to get back to the others now, if you don't mind." He held the door open for Everley because there was no way he'd risk Everley going over to the window to investigate.

Everley discovering Louisa beneath his open window was hardly what that family needed.

"If you change your mind," Everley started as they entered the hall.

"I won't."

The other man seemed to be at a loss for words, a pleasant sight after his insufferable smugness just moments ago.

"If you'll excuse me, I must go." *I must go strangle my bride-to-be.*

He left Everley in the billiard room with some gentlemen friends before rushing off.

It took him less than a minute to make his way outside and around the side of the house, just in time to see Louisa brushing dirt off her skirts as she came to stand.

"What on earth were you thinking?" he growled as he came upon her. "You could have been caught. You could have been *ruined.*"

Her eyes were impossibly wide and too dark for him to read in the shadows. Her voice, however—that was easy enough to decipher. It was filled with hurt and outrage as she said, "You're going to marry her."

"What?" he snapped. "Who?"

"You're going to marry Margaret after you promised me you weren't going to." She sniffed and he realized with a dangerous tightness in his chest that she was *crying.*

Oh Lord, spare him from Louisa's tears.

They did something to him. Something he hated. It made him feel desperate, which was likely why he went speechless. He gaped at her for a long moment before finally managing, "Are you *daft?*"

She blinked in surprise, but at least that was better than tears. "Pardon me?" she sniffed with affront.

He exhaled loudly as he reached for her, drawing her out of the dirt and back toward the lawn. "I asked to court you. I told you I have no interest in Margaret—"

"Yes, but you said—"

"I said I'd marry Torrent's daughter, I didn't say which one," he said, his voice sharper than he'd intended.

"Oh." She stopped walking. "*Oh.*"

He rolled his eyes heavenward. "Yes. *Oh.*"

"But he said—"

"Yes, well, Everley said a lot of things, not one of which were meant for your ears." He turned to her with a meaningful glare.

She had the good grace to blush, at least, though she did not apologize for eavesdropping. "So, does that mean you intend..."

He stared at her. This could not be happening. He hadn't expected an ordinary courtship with such an extraordinary girl, but even so, surely he was not about to have this conversation like...this.

She tilted her head to the side. "Does that mean you plan to marry me?"

Oh for the love of— "That is the plan, yes."

Her mouth fell open as she gaped at him. Here, in the dark of night, beside the house of the man who'd love nothing more than to find some sort of leverage over him.

"Could this conversation wait until we'd ensured your reputation has not been utterly destroyed?" he asked.

She didn't appear to hear him. "So when you said you wished to court me..." She blinked dazedly. "You were very serious."

"Deadly serious." He met her gaze evenly and for a heartbeat his irritation with her was tempered by tenderness. What on earth had her family done to her to make it so dashedly difficult for her to see her own worth?

"Why?"

Oh, for heaven's sake. "Why *what*?"

"Why me? Why not Margaret?"

How was it possible to find her so very appealing while also so very irritating? Even so, he found that his affection won out, and he managed to ask mildly, "Haven't we been over this already?"

She shook her head. "No."

"I..." He heard a noise coming. A giggle and laugh. People moving in the shrubbery. Blast it all, if they did not move quickly they could be caught and then the lengthy, proper, perfect courtship he'd had planned would be replaced by a hasty, embarrassed shotgun wedding.

No, thank you. Not on his watch.

"Come along, Louisa," he said quietly, tugging on her arm as he led her toward a side door.

"Please just tell me why—"

"I prefer you," he growled, not even bothering to hide his irritation. "Now get in there."

He shoved her inside the door none-too-gently before slamming it shut behind her.

In the silence that followed, he blinked up at the night sky.

Well, that had...not gone according to plan.

He straightened his cravat as he headed toward the sound of revelers in the garden. Since he'd kissed Louisa earlier, his head had been spinning with the romantic ways she deserved to be wooed, courted, and then proposed to.

And just like that he'd ruined them all.

*I prefer you...*

Yes, that was precisely the eloquent sonnet she deserved. He sighed and shook his head as he turned the corner and re-entered the fray. He'd certainly have to try and do better than that the next time he saw her if he stood any chance of making her fall for him the way he was losing his wits over her.

He snatched up a champagne glass and downed it in one go. He'd talk to her father first, and then, he'd set in place a plan of action.

Once she was thoroughly smitten, he would propose to her.

Again.
Though next time he'd do better. *I prefer you.*
Heaven knew he couldn't do much worse.

# 13

Delilah's nose was wrinkled delicately in distaste, like she'd just smelled something sour. "He said he *prefers* you?"

"Those exact words?" Prudence added.

Louisa nodded.

"How did he say it?" Addie asked.

Louisa sighed. "He sort of shouted it at me."

"In a pleasant manner?" Prudence asked, confusion written all over her face.

Louisa shook her head. It hadn't been pleasant at all. It might have been if she hadn't been such a turkey. Eavesdropping and spying and then accusing him of lying about his intentions.

She picked at some lint on her skirt as she stewed in her own misery. If he hadn't come to his sense about her earlier in the night, he must have realized it now. She wasn't fit to be his wife, and definitely not adequate marchioness material.

"Well, that is...nice," Addie said hesitantly.

Delilah wrinkled her brow at Addie in clear disbelief. "He

said he preferred her. As if she was the least objectionable option. Hardly swoonworthy now is it?"

"But the things he said earlier on the balcony," Prudence interrupted. "That was rather lovely."

She hadn't told them about the kiss. Not even Addie. The kiss was her secret. It wasn't often she had a real fantasy to carry around with her and that kiss was one she cherished.

Every other moment of the evening, however, had been subject to an intense amount of scrutiny—by herself and her friends. Less than twenty-four hours had passed and a large portion of that had been spent rehashing his words.

"I still cannot believe you tried to eavesdrop outside Everley's window," Addie said with a sigh. Reggie in her lap laughed as though this news was a joke.

"I told you, I had to," Louisa said.

Addie tilted her head to the side, her gaze filled with disbelief. "Did you, though?"

Louisa sniffed as she reached for a sugary treat from the box that Tolston had sent over for Addie. "I wish you would let that part go, already."

"I wish you'd learned more while you were out there," Prudence said.

They all turned to her in surprise and Prudence shrugged. "What? If she was risking her neck to find out something scandalous about Lord Everley, I wish she'd learnt more than what we could already have surmised."

Louisa's brows arched. "You knew that Everley held my father's debts?"

"Do not be so crass." Prudence shifted noisily. "I merely meant that your family's financial troubles are not a secret—"

"They aren't?"

Prudence's answering look held a note of pity. "Everley's involvement is interesting but not criminal."

"Why, Prudence," Delilah teased. "When did you become an expert on what is criminal?"

Prudence sniffed in that superior way of hers. "Do not be ridiculous. You all knew what I meant."

"Indeed," Addie said. "Although, knowing that he uses his power to manipulate and control, this could help the investigation."

"See?" Louisa said brightly.

All three of the other ladies shot her a glare in return. It seemed even these three diverse women were all of one mind when it came to Louisa's eavesdropping, and that was that she should not have done it.

Louisa was inclined to agree, if she were being honest.

Things between her and Tumberland had ended so nicely after that kiss.

*That kiss.*

Was it possible she was still swooning over a kiss?

Yes. She absolutely was. Her eyes fluttered shut as she allowed herself another moment to revel in the way he'd looked at her just before he'd closed his lips over hers...

"Did you hear me, Louisa?" Delilah asked.

Louisa's eyes snapped open. "Uh..."

"I said you must be thrilled." The way Delilah said it sounded less jubilant than inquisitive. The others were all giving her a similar look.

"To have a marquess who wishes to court you..." Prudence looked at her carefully. Almost warily. "That is rather...unexpected. Is it not?"

*Oh drat.* "You all don't believe he means it either!"

"No, no," Addie said quickly. "That's not it at all."

Louisa shook her head. "Of course you don't. Why would he want me—?"

"Oh please," Delilah said with a roll of her eyes. "Enough with that. I could very easily understand him wanting you.

*Preferring* you even." She gestured toward Louisa with one hand. "You might not resemble your sister, but you are beautiful in your own right."

Louisa blinked. "I am?"

She stared at Delilah for a long moment, waiting for the other girl to laugh. Delilah was not one to say nice things to be nice. She wasn't really one to say nice things, period.

So, if she said it, then she most likely believed it to be true.

"Of course you are," Prudence said with disdain.

Louisa blinked in surprise at that. "If that is true... If you believe he might genuinely prefer me, then why are you all looking at me like that?"

Addie looked to the others and then back to her. "We're just concerned, that's all."

Louisa's brows hitched up. "That a marquess has taken an interest in me?"

"That you might feel *beholden...*" she started.

"That you might have reservations," Prudence added delicately.

Delilah scoffed openly at their attempts at diplomacy. "We want to make sure you're all right with it, is all. We know you'd do what you must for your family, but no one wants to see you miserable."

It took her much too long to make out what they were trying to say. "You think *I'd* be miserable?" Her mind flashed to the handsome man who'd turned her world upside down. "Why?"

Addie scrunched up her nose. "Well, he's just so..."

"Boring," Delilah said.

"Uppity," Prudence hedged, her voice a question.

Addie nodded. "You said yourself he was insufferable."

"Yes, but..." *I'd been wrong.* The words didn't come. Possibly because they weren't entirely true. He *was* all those things...and yet he wasn't at all. With her, alone, he was so very different. So much more than she'd first suspected after their first fateful run-in.

Addie was watching her expectantly, waiting for a response.

*Had* she called him insufferable? Guilt had her shifting under Addie's stare. "I only said that after the ghost incident," she said, as if that would explained matters. "It's possible I judged too harshly."

"The ghost incident?" Delilah repeated in rightful confusion. Louisa never had told Delilah and Prudence about that night.

Addie waved aside the question. "But do you *like* him, Louisa?" she asked, her gaze fixed on her with something akin to suspicion.

"I..." She cleared her throat. '*Like*' felt like such a pale, insipid word for what she felt when she was around him. She didn't like him, no. Whatever this was...it was far more intense and vivid and passionate and...and...*confusing*.

She thought back to his kiss, to the way he'd spoken to her—like she was somebody worth speaking to. Like she was someone worth thinking about. Like she was somebody worth kissing.

Yes, she'd definitely developed a one-track mind when it came to kissing.

"I wish I could see him again," she said with a sigh.

They all stared in surprise at that. It was the only truth she knew for certain. Her head had been reeling ever since he'd kissed her and she wasn't sure what to make of anything. "I want to see him again." She said it with more conviction this time.

"If he truly plans to court you, I'm certain you will," Prudence said.

*If.* Louisa's insides flinched at her use of the word 'if.'

So, she wasn't the only one who doubted all he'd said. She wasn't the only one who thought it sounded too good to be true.

"Of course she'll see him again," Delilah said. "I wouldn't be surprised if he came to visiting hours to pay his respects," she said.

"Do you think he will?" Louisa asked.

"Definitely," Addie said, leaning over to squeeze her hand reassuringly.

Louisa smiled. Of course. If he were in earnest, surely he'd come to see her. Wouldn't he?

Yes, he would.

Two more days passed and he...did not.

Her mother and sister did, however.

She found herself sitting rather painfully in the formal drawing room, the situation so very similar to their last visit and yet utterly new.

Because now she knew that the marquess wanted her.

Or at least she thought he did.

She hoped he did.

She just hoped he hadn't changed his mind.

Her belly flipped at the thought.

It didn't help that her mother was still so very certain that Tumberland was meant for Margaret. "He's expected tomorrow, you know," she said with a sly little look at her eldest daughter.

Margaret didn't acknowledge the glance.

"Did you, uh..." Louisa took a deep breath as guilt mixed with embarrassment. "Er, that is...Margaret, did you enjoy your evening? Did you enjoy...Lord Tumberland?"

Margaret blushed.

Louisa frowned.

What did that blush mean? Louisa had been blushing

nonstop, as well, since the party the other night, but that was because he'd *kissed* her.

He hadn't kissed Margaret as well, had he?

She huffed with impatience at herself. She'd had little faith in Tumberland and his feelings from the start, but days of silence on his end had managed to drive her to distraction.

Margaret eyed her oddly as she answered. "Yes, I had a lovely evening, thank you."

"Well, of course she did." Her mother shifted in her seat. "He danced with her *twice*." Somehow this sounded like she was arguing. As though Louisa had claimed he'd only danced with her once.

"Yes, but—"

Her mother's eyes narrowed. Margaret's gaze grew curious. Even Miss Grayson was watching her with her teacup halfway to her lips as though worried about what she might say next.

"Might I have a word with you in private, Margaret?" she managed. Now she, too, was blushing furiously and never in her life had she been embarrassed to speak to her own sister.

All the other ladies exchanged a baffled look, but Margaret quickly set her tea to the side. "Of course, Lulu."

*Lulu*. The old nickname seemed to taunt her now. She and her sister might not have been close, but they were still sisters and she was about to break her sister's heart.

Wasn't she?

Oh, of course she was.

Who wouldn't be head over heels in love with the marquess? Oh certainly, he seemed a bit intimidating and standoffish at first glance, but anyone who'd spent any time with the man would be won over by that mischievous glint in his eyes, in the way he looked at you like you were the only person on the planet.

Louisa led the way out into the gardens behind the school

and waited until her sister had found a seat on a bench before she started. "Margaret, would you be very disappointed if Tumberland was not preparing to court you?"

The words came out in a rush of inelegance that made Louisa cringe. For once she wished she knew the right thing to say that did not involve putting her foot in her mouth.

Margaret studied her closely. "What is it that you think you know, Louisa?"

"Um..." *He kissed me. He says he wishes to court me instead. We had a moment, you see... Or at least, I thought we had, but truth be told it feels more like a dream now...*

The longer her silence lasted the more certain she was that she'd gotten it all wrong. She'd somehow misunderstood.

It had been just another misunderstanding. One of the many that made up the course of her ridiculous life.

Margaret reached out and squeezed her hand. "Dear, you ought not look so distraught."

"But—"

"I'd be relieved," Margaret said. She'd said it so quickly that Louisa thought perhaps she'd misheard.

"You'd...*what?*"

Margaret winced as she tugged at her gloves. "Do not tell Mother."

"No, of course not," Louisa was quick to reassure her. "I would never."

Margaret sighed, and the sound seemed to echo in the trees as a brisk breeze made the leaves flutter around them. "It is not that Tumberland is so very awful..."

"No, of course not," Louisa said again, this time with a scowl. Awful? Were they still discussing Tumberland? Certainly not, because who on earth would think him awful? The man was odd, certainly, for preferring Louisa to Margaret, but other than that quirk, he was really quite perfect.

A memory of warm, dazzlingly golden eyes had her holding her breath. For a second, she thought she could smell the distinct, heady scent of his cologne. She bit her lip to stop the wistful ache that was starting to feel like a permanent fixture in her chest.

It was stupid.

Impossible, even.

No one missed a man they barely knew and had only recently met. That was insanity.

"Do not misunderstand," Margaret was saying now, her cheeks still pink and her expression oddly flustered. "Were Tumberland to propose, I would undoubtedly say yes."

Louisa clenched her fists. The very thought of *her* man proposing to Margaret—not that he *was* hers. Not yet. But try telling that to the churning jealousy that would not be denied.

Margaret's sad sigh brought her back to the moment and helped her remember herself. "But he has *not* mentioned marriage to you," Louisa confirmed.

Margaret shot her a questioning look before shaking her head.

Louisa didn't try to hide her sigh of relief. She knew what he'd said. She reminded herself of it daily, but she couldn't stop the fact that while she wanted to believe in whatever magic it was that had come over him the other night—she couldn't quite convince herself, especially not here in the cold light of day.

"Mother expects that he'll talk to Father tomorrow," Margaret said. "And after that he will talk to me."

Louisa let out a long exhale. That sounded...reasonable. She wished it didn't also sound so very predictable. She wished she couldn't see it happening in her mind's eye, exactly as her mother and sister and father all seemed to think it would.

Of all the times for her fanciful imagination to quit on her, it would have to be now.

Margaret was staring down at her lap. "The truth is..."

Louisa waited miserably for her sister to expand on the future she had planned with the marquess.

"The truth is, I prefer his friend."

Louisa's head snapped up as Margaret's hand clamped over her own mouth as if she'd horrified herself by speaking aloud.

"What?" Louisa breathed.

Margaret's eyes widened to saucers on her pretty face and she gave her head a little shake. "I shouldn't have said that," she mumbled through her gloved hand.

Louisa blinked wildly. Maybe Margaret shouldn't have said it, but she had. Relief flooded her at the realization that Margaret wasn't even remotely besotted with Tumberland.

"You like Mr. Allen," she said with a laugh.

Margaret turned red and scowled at her. "This is not amusing."

"It is, though." But she cut herself short. A part of her wanted to explain everything, but she couldn't. Not yet.

She wished to say that she would marry Tumberland and that all would be well, but here in the light of day sitting next to her perfect sister...the words would not come. They seemed like the worst sort of lie.

She could only imagine her sister's look of shock and disbelief, which would be nothing compared to her mother's.

"Margaret," she said, reaching out a hand to cover her sister's. "Trust me when I say that we will find another way to save this family."

Her sister shook her head, tears welling up in her eyes. "You don't know the half of it, Lulu."

Louisa squeezed her sister's hand. She knew more than Margaret realized, thanks to her spying efforts. She wondered if even Margaret knew just how dire their family's financial difficulties were. Or that it was Lord Evil who was forcing their father's hand.

She only wished anything she'd overheard might have helped Tolston create a criminal argument against that cruel man. But being cruel wasn't necessarily against the law and it did nothing to prove he was conspiring with would-be murderers or dastardly guardians.

"I promise you, Margaret, all will be well," she said.

Her sister's eyes were full of hope—she wanted to believe her, that much was clear.

"Tumberland will...Tumberland has..." She couldn't bring herself to finish.

Tumberland...what? Tumberland had kissed her. He'd said some pretty words about courtship and preferring her, whatever that meant. That was hardly enough to reassure her family and keep them safe.

And in the days that had passed he'd done nothing to make good on his words. She hadn't heard from him, hadn't seen him...

"Yes," Margaret said, patting her hand kindly as she stood. "I'm sure Tumberland *will*."

Her sister looked so resigned, her smile so sad and her air so final, Louisa couldn't bring herself to argue.

Margaret expected him to propose to her and right at this particular moment, it seemed like the logical assumption. To suggest any alternative seemed like tempting fate. It would be cruel to give her sister false hope.

Oh, who was she fooling? *She* was the one who did not wish to harbor false hopes. It was her heart that would be crushed if she let herself believe and then had her hopes dashed.

"Will we see you tomorrow?" Margaret asked.

Louisa opened her mouth and closed it promptly. Her

mother had not invited her to dinner with Tumberland and his friend. The only way she would be invited was if Tumberland forced them to invite her...again.

That thought added to her sadness as she forced a smile. "I doubt it."

Margaret seemed to understand and her answering smile was just as sad. "I'm sorry, Lulu. You know our parents love you, it is just—"

"I understand," she said. And she did. The mature part of her knew very well that they cared about her, but that she'd embarrassed them in the past and couldn't risk that now.

She understood.

She did.

The sound of the leaves rustling behind her made her sigh. *This is reality*, they seemed to say. She might have been lost in a dream the other night, but then again—Tumberland might have been as well.

Perhaps he'd been in his cups.

He hadn't *seemed* it, but then again, she wasn't familiar with the signs.

"Now you look worried," Margaret said. "I did not mean to cause you concern."

"Do not be daft, Margaret," she said affectionately. "This is my family, too. All of your concerns are mine, as well. I know I've always been..." They shared a look as Louisa struggled for the right word. "Eccentric."

Her sister smiled softly. "Believe it or not, I wouldn't have you any other way."

"Yes, well, I am sorry if that added more pressure for you to be perfect," she said.

Margaret blinked rapidly. "You did nothing wrong, dear. I was always glad that you were able to keep your childish way."

Louisa tried not to wince but Margaret must have seen

her because her smile was soft and sad. "I did not mean it that way, Louisa."

"No, it's all right," she said. "I understand. I've never been asked to make a sacrifice for this family. But perhaps it is time that I did."

For once in her life, she needed to stop being childish. Stop believing in fantasies and miracles and start thinking about what would be best for her family and her sister. If that meant she had to release Tumberland from whatever madness had made him kiss her and make promises he was likely reconsidering...then that was what she would do.

Margaret eyed her warily. "Why do you have that look in your eyes?"

"Do I have a look?" she asked mildly.

Margaret pursed her lips. "You know that you do. It strikes fear in my heart whenever I see it."

Louisa patted her sister's shoulder. "No need to be afraid, Margaret. In fact, I mean to make everything better."

Margaret sighed. "But you see, Sister, there really is no need. It has already been done."

"What has?"

"Tumberland is supposed to talk to Father tomorrow. Mother and Father fully expect a proposal."

Louisa stared at her. Maybe he *had* changed his mind, and if he had?

Then she would be okay with it.

Eventually.

She swallowed down a stabbing pain.

Oh, all right, maybe she'd never be able to be happy for her sister, but she would do her best to step aside gracefully.

This time the wind in the trees behind her felt less reassuring and far more ominous.

"We'd better go back inside," Margaret said. "Mother will be wondering what we're talking about."

Louisa forced a smile. She'd caused a scene for nothing, because when push came to shove she couldn't figure out how to tell her sister that the man everyone thought she'd marry had kissed her instead. That he preferred her.

Her heart wanted to hold onto those words, but her brain chose this particular moment to embrace pragmatism. Pretty words after a gentleman got carried away and kissed a girl in the shadows paled in comparison to plans that all of society expected to see realized.

This time the wind snapped a twig behind her and she jumped before giving her head a little shake to rid herself of silly thoughts of ghosts and spirits. That sensation she used to get when she imagined Sir Edmond watching her was back in full force now, and her skin prickled with the feeling of being watched.

Glancing over her shoulder as she followed Margaret inside, she told herself she was being ridiculous. There was nothing there but wind and—

She stopped short, her eyes going wide and her mouth forming a little *O* as her gaze collided with Tumberland's. He was standing behind a tree and his oh-so-serious expression never changed as he lifted a finger to his lips to tell her to keep quiet.

"Are you coming, Louisa?" Margaret called back.

"Yes—yes! I'm coming." She frowned at Tumberland in confusion as she backed away. She held a finger up in a gesture that she meant to say, *give me a moment*. And then she turned and headed back inside—more confused than ever.

# 14

This was not his finest hour.

Hiding in the garden of his intended was definitely one of the more ridiculous situations in which Lawrence had ever found himself. Sneaking into the school's gardens might not have been *the* stupidest thing he'd ever done, but it was certainly up there in the top ten.

All right, fine. The top five.

But he'd wanted to see her. He'd needed to see her.

Alone.

He hadn't expected to see her quite so suddenly, or in these very gardens. Truth be told, he'd been seeking ways to climb the trellis to her room, when she and her sister had stepped outside.

Her sister was right. She *had* gotten a look. A look he recognized as surely as her sister did. She'd looked determined.

Uneasiness spread through him and what he'd thought to be a romantic plan now seemed...pathetic, really.

What if he'd gotten it all wrong? He'd assumed she'd felt this thing between them as well but what if she was just determined to help her family, to save her sister from being the sacrificial lamb?

He scowled at the tree trunk beside him. He *was* a prize catch, was he not?

And yet, Margaret had clearly stated she wanted his best friend, Gregory, and Louisa...

Well, that was the question, wasn't it?

What did Louisa want?

He'd shocked her with a kiss and then had fairly bitten her head off when he'd caught her eavesdropping. Not to mention the fact that she'd clearly had her mind filled with all the threats and gossip that Lord Everley had thrown about so carelessly.

And then she'd heard about his intentions to marry through a window.

He drew in a deep breath and let it out slowly. This was just about the most mixed-up courtship he'd ever heard of, and it hadn't even properly begun.

When she appeared in the garden a moment later, he no longer had surprise on his side, but he did have the thick grove of trees behind which he stood. He let himself enjoy the moment as she looked around for him.

He let himself enjoy *her*. He'd missed her, and the sight of her now was a salve to that homesick ache. Three days had felt like a lifetime when it meant being away from the woman he loved. Staying away had been torture.

When she spotted him, her eyes narrowed and she rushed forward. "What are you doing here?"

"I wished to speak with you," he said.

She stopped just shy of touching him, her hand reaching out and hovering awkwardly before she seemed to think better of her brazen actions and called her hand back to her side.

Pity. Everything in him ached to feel her touch again.

But her grim determination earlier gave him pause.

Was his ego easily bruised? He'd never have thought so prior to meeting this young lady. But she was like no woman he'd ever met before and her opinion mattered more than anyone's.

He'd assumed that the things that mattered to others didn't seem to matter to her; but what if he'd thought wrong?

"Was there a reason you've come to spy on me in the back garden?" she asked now, wariness in her eyes and in her voice as her gaze raked over him.

"I was not spying," he said stiffly.

He had been spying.

"Not intentionally," he added more truthfully.

Her lips seemed to twitch with amusement even as her brows drew together in a question. "Were you hoping to hear Margaret speak?"

"No," he said quickly. "I hadn't even realized she'd be here."

"So, you just snuck into these gardens..."

"To see you," he finished. "I wanted a moment alone before I talk to your father tomorrow."

"I see." She blinked quickly and then her expression went blank.

"I highly doubt you do," he murmured.

The silence between them grew thick.

"Why would you wish to see me alone?" She turned away. "If you've had a change of heart—"

"I have not."

She stilled but did not turn back. He placed a hand on her shoulder and nudged. He needed to see her face. "If *you* have—"

"I haven't." She whipped around so suddenly, he found her in his arms. He wasn't sure who'd moved first but now that she was there, he wasn't letting go.

She still looked anxious, though, and that made him nervous. "I heard you and your sister," he said.

She blinked and then started nibbling on her lower lip in such a way that he knew he'd think of little else but her lips for the rest of the day. "Then I suppose you realize she does not...prefer you."

He wasn't sure if she was trying to tease but he suspected by the glint of amusement in her eyes that she was.

He found a smile tugging at his lips despite the dilemma that overheard conversation brought up for him. "Yes, well...I suppose my pride will survive."

"You do not mind then?" she asked.

He just barely held back a sigh. "Why would I mind when I've already made my choice."

Her cheeks turned a stunning shade of pink, and happiness made her eyes glow. "But it occurred to me while listening to you both..." He cleared his throat. "I have made my feelings clear."

"Your preference?" she asked just a little too mildly.

He growled in agreement and watched her stifle a laugh.

"And Margaret has stated *her* preference," he continued. He trailed off meaningfully but rather than respond, Louisa just blinked up at him.

"Was there a point you wished to make, my lord?" she asked.

"Lawrence," he said. "Please, call me Lawrence."

Her smile was small and so unbearably sweet. So unbelievably genuine. The most real thing he'd ever seen in his life. And yet... He had to be certain.

"It occurred to me that you have not made *your* preference clear."

She stared at him for a long moment before her brows shot up in understanding. "Oh, you mean...do I...er...do I have a preference for you?"

The heat in her cheeks warmed his chest, because he felt almost certain it meant that she did. He reached for her hands and she did not try to pull away. Another good sign, he figured. "I do not wish for you to feel trapped," he said, his voice gruff. Years of not discussing emotions had left him rusty. He cleared his throat. "I heard you say that you would do what it takes to save your family and I need you to know that I would not force your hand."

She widened her eyes and he was almost certain he'd drown in them if he did not look away. How could any one person look so very sincere all the time? Had no one ever taught her to hide her feelings?

He was grateful no one had, but looking at her now, like this—so open, so youthful, so naïve and brave and strong and fragile...

He felt the urge to toss her over his shoulder and whisk her away. To keep her safe forever, even though he had more than a little suspicion that she was stronger and more intuitively intelligent than anyone ever gave her credit.

Even now, she didn't stammer or hem and haw. If anything, she seemed entertained by him and his question.

"What would you do if I said I was not interested in a romantic relationship with you?" she asked, tilting her head to the side.

"I'd buy the plot of land from your father and give him a loan until he could get out from under Everley's grasp."

She blinked. "Just like that."

"Just like that," he said.

He'd be crushed. But he wouldn't tell her that. He'd meant it when he'd said he wanted her to have freedom to choose. He might not have known Louisa for long, but he knew with a deep certainty that the only thing that could truly hurt this joyful, free soul was to be entrapped in a marriage she did not want.

Her gaze never wavered, but her lips curved up and up and up, until she was giving him the most brilliant smile he'd ever seen. Leaning forward, her voice dropped to a whisper. "And that," she said with a hushed reverence that made him grin. "That is why *I* prefer *you*."

The breath he'd been holding left him in a *whoosh* of relief. "You are sure."

"I'm as certain as I can be considering I barely know you."

He tugged her hands and she tripped forward, the weight of her crushing against his chest as he wrapped his arms around her tight. "That was why I came here today. I want to spend time with you...alone. I want us to know each other."

"So you decided to sneak into the gardens," she said with a laugh.

"Actually, I had every intention of sneaking up to your bedroom."

Her eyes grew wide. "Oh."

A joy he'd never felt before made it impossible to stop grinning at her shock...and her obvious pleasure at the idea.

"What happened?" she asked, turning to eye the brick wall that held no trellis and was nowhere near a tree to climb. "Ah."

"Yes. Ah," he agreed sorrowfully. It had been a remarkably romantic idea, if he did say so himself. It was just better in theory than in practicality.

"You know you could just join us for calling hours," she said.

"Yes, but I was hoping to see...*that*."

She drew her brows together. "What?"

With one finger he lightly traced the curve of her lips. "This."

She blinked rapidly, her breath on his finger coming in short bursts. "You wanted to see me smile?"

"Very badly," he admitted.

Her smile grew and he was certain he'd never been more proud.

"Tell me something no one else knows about you," she said. Her eyes sparkled with happiness.

"You're not going to believe it." He shook his head ruefully. "No one would."

She bit her lip as if to stifle a laugh, as if laughter were her default setting and was ready to bubble up at a moment's notice. "Try me."

"I've fallen victim to love at first sight."

Her eyes widened playfully as a smile curved her lips. "No," she said with a shocked gasp.

"It's true." His voice was mild as ever as he told her the tale. "You see I was bored silly at a house party—"

"Something which I would be sure *never* to tell my mother," she murmured.

"And I was just heading inside to go to sleep, when you will never guess what I saw..."

Her cheeks started to pinken as she grinned up at him. "A vision of beauty and grace?" she suggested.

"Exactly!" He reached out and brushed some hair back from her face—an excuse to touch her, really. "You see, this vision of loveliness was dancing alone. And that..." He tsked loudly. "That would not do."

"Oh no?"

"No." He made his expression severe and she giggled.

"And here I thought you mistook this vision of loveliness for a child."

His lips quirked up. *Touché*. "For a moment, yes. From behind, with her hair braided and her nightgown trailing the floor, the little sprite looked a bit like a child. But then I held her in my arms..."

Her smile softened and grew so sweet it made his chest ache with tenderness. "Oh yes?"

He leaned down. "Trust me, there was no mistaking the fact that she was a grown lady once I held her in my arms."

"Oh." She said it as a sigh.

He drew her into his arms now, as if they were once more going to dance together. "She was definitely *not* a child," he said. "But she had the most magical ability to retain a child-like sense of passion and magic."

"Did she now?" she murmured. Her eyes were dazed as he leaned forward slightly. She blinked and her smile turned rueful. "Some would say she was prone to mischief and trouble."

"Or," he said. "Some might say she was brave and unexpected. Nothing about her was predictable or muted."

"Muted?" She pulled back slightly in surprise.

"Don't you think most people are muted?"

She pursed her lips as she thought that over. "Perhaps."

"But not her."

"No?" Her smile was teasing, her eyes filled with joy.

"Everything about her is vivid, warm, and filled with life." He'd long since dropped his teasing tone and he could only hope she saw his utter sincerity now as he looked down at her.

Judging by her thick swallow and the tears that brimmed her eyes, she was catching on. "Wow," she said softly. "This lady sounds..." She shook her head at a loss for words.

"Special," he finished just as quietly. "Unique. One of a kind..."

Her tears overflowed now and she shook her head with a laugh as he used a thumb to brush one away. "I am sorry. I don't know what's come over me. I'm never such a watering pot."

"Never apologize for your emotions," he said gruffly. "In fact, if it were up to me, you would never apologize for your actions, either."

She bit her lip. "Not even when I've been shamelessly eavesdropping?"

He laughed under his breath. He'd overreacted and he knew it. But in his defense, he'd been so worried about what could have happened to her if she'd been caught. If it had been Everley and not he who'd found her in the dirt, who'd realized all she might have heard out there under that window...

He shook his head. "I was angry that you did not keep yourself safe. But I hope soon, in the not too distant future, keeping you safe will be my honor."

She made a funny little face in return. "I can take care of myself."

"Says the girl who toppled out a window," he shot back.

She shrugged. "I wouldn't have broken anything if you hadn't caught me."

"Fair enough," he said. "But might we agree that you are perhaps too quick to act without thinking through repercussions?"

She narrowed her eyes as she thought that over. "I'll allow that perhaps I do not always use the best judgment."

He rewarded that bit of honesty with a quick kiss that had her eyes sparkling up at him when he pulled back. "I do have a question, though."

"And what is that?"

She wrapped her arms around his neck and the simple gesture made his heart swell so large in his chest he thought he might perish from this happiness. "If your duty in this relationship is to keep me safe...what is my task?"

He tightened his grip on her waist. Could she not see yet just how much he needed her? No one else. Only her. "You, my little love, are tasked with the arduous duty of ensuring I don't get too serious. That I don't get so lost in my obligations and day-to-day duties that I forget to see the beauty and the magic of the world around me."

Her smile softened as her expression turned thoughtful. "That I can do."

"I know you can," he said. "You have from the moment I met you."

She went up on tiptoe and pressed her lips to his in a kiss that was perfect and sweet.

He tightened his grip and tilted his head, at long last letting himself give in to temptation and kiss her thoroughly the way he'd been dying to do from the very first time he saw her.

The sound of the back door opening and Louisa's name being called broke through his happy haze, and he pulled back regretfully. "I should leave," he said. "They will be looking for you."

She nodded with a sigh. "I suppose we must part."

"Tomorrow," he said. "Come to your parents' house tomorrow."

Her smile was bittersweet. "I was not invited."

A surge of anger made him long to shake her father and then her mother until they finally saw what they'd been blessed with in Louisa. The beautiful rare gem that was right in front of their faces. He cupped her precious face in his palms as he leaned down and dropped a kiss on her nose. "You will be welcome."

Her smile was sudden and bright. "You seem awfully certain of that."

He laughed. "That's because I *am* certain." Once he informed her father that Louisa was to be his wife, a marchioness, the savior of the family's financial difficulties, and one of the wealthiest and most powerful ladies in the land... Well, he was quite certain Louisa would never feel unwelcome in any home ever again.

"Louisa, are you out here?" a girl's voice shouted. "Reggie is looking for you."

Her face brightened so beautifully he had to fight a sudden and silly surge of jealousy. "Reggie?" he asked. "Who is Reggie?"

"He is my dearest friend," Louisa said. Her smile turned mischievous as she backed away. "He's loyal and sweet, and I'd say he'd give you a run for your money on claiming my heart if he did not drool so very often."

"Drool...?" he repeated. And then a young child was shouting "Lulu!" into the treetops and she giggled.

"Go," he said with a laugh. "And tell this Reggie that he may be your friend, but your heart and your hand have been claimed by another."

Her cheeks flushed pink as her smile spread to become an impossibly wide grin as she reached the edge of the trees. "Until tomorrow?"

"Until tomorrow," he said.

# 15

Tomorrow could not come quickly enough.

Twenty-four excruciatingly long hours passed, with much help from her friends, thank goodness, but in all that time to prepare, she still was not quite ready when she showed up on the doorstep of her parents' rented townhome.

Louisa wasn't certain what she was expecting upon her arrival, but if it had involved being welcomed into the family home with open arms...

Her hopes were dashed quickly.

"Louisa, what are you doing here?" her mother asked in a melodramatically hushed voice, as if a stage whisper would help to hide the fact that Louisa was here, in their drawing room, waiting like a visitor for someone to acknowledge her presence.

"Well, I—"

"Lulu, I'm so glad you're here." Margaret's smile was strained as she entered the room, but at least her sister had said the polite thing.

Maybe she'd even meant it. After all, Margaret had actually trusted her with the truth yesterday, and Louisa could hardly wait until she had a moment alone with her sister to tell her that she was off the hook, so to speak.

Not that marrying Tumberland was a hook.

Far from it.

Tumberland had turned out to be her very own dream come true. Just the thought made her giddy. All those years of dreaming about some noble, stoic, upright man who thought she was perfect just the way she was...

Even *she* hadn't quite been able to believe that her personal fairytale could come true.

And if anyone had told her just a few weeks ago that he would come in the form of the oh-so-proper Tumberland, well...

She sighed happily, lost in her own pleasant thoughts until her mother snapped her out of it.

Literally.

Her mother snapped fingers in front of her face.

"What is wrong with you, Louisa? Are you suffering from a fever? You look *delusional*." Her mother's words wiped some of her happiness from her face, but not her heart.

She clung to Tumberland's words from the day before with all her might. Maybe one day she would not need his reassurances to feel confident in herself, but until then...she took heart in the fact that she trusted him.

Why?

She had no idea. She didn't know him well enough to trust him. That was what her mind said, but her heart and her instincts rebelled. She *trusted* him. And despite what logic might state, she *knew* him.

Every time she'd looked in his eyes, she'd known it as surely as she knew her name was Louisa.

She *knew* him.

Crazy as it might be, she knew him in a way no one else

seemed to. Like she'd been given a magical looking glass that revealed the true Tumberland.

*Lawrence.*

He'd told her to call him Lawrence and it was about time she started.

"The marquess is here," her mother hissed. "Now is not the time for a visit, silly girl."

"Mother, she could not have known," Margaret chastened quietly.

Louisa looked from one to the other. She had known. It was the reason she was here. But she had no desire to argue with her mother or explain that he wanted her here.

"Is he..." She cleared her throat and tried again, as nerves were getting the better of her. "Is he with Father?"

That was all it took to make her mother forget her anger in lieu of outright excitement. It made Margaret's skin pale so drastically, Louisa worried she might faint.

"Margaret," she said quietly. "Perhaps we could have a word alone—"

"Absolutely not," her mother snapped. "Margaret must be available to speak to Tumberland alone the moment he's done with your father."

"Yes, but—"

"Do not argue, Louisa," her mother interjected.

"But—" She was about to argue further when the sound of male voices had all three ladies shooting desperate glances toward the door.

The voices were her father's and Tumberland's and they were growing ever louder as they drew closer.

Louisa felt a surge of inexplicable nerves. How had her father responded? What would her mother say? Would Margaret feel betrayed?

Worse, would anyone even believe that he wanted her? That thought turned nerves into panic. She was not ready to face her family's disbelief, not when she was only now beginning to trust in this newfound love.

Her heart raced. Her stomach churned. As the door opened, the panic became unbearable. That was the only excuse she could come up with later for her actions.

She ducked.

When her father and Tumberland entered the room she dove behind the settee.

It was beyond ridiculous and she found herself staring up at the ceiling in abject humiliation as all voices went silent and her mind went blank.

A heartbeat passed and then the most handsome, dear face in the world came into view above her, blocking her view of the crown molding.

A small smile tugged at Lawrence's lips and his eyes danced with laughter as he reached a hand out to help her up. "Ah, here she is now," he said mildly, as though it were not at all unusual to find her sprawled on the floor, hiding from her own family.

"Louisa, whatever are you doing?" her mother hissed.

She was vaguely aware of her father reaching out to her mother, trying to stop her.

"Please excuse Louisa, my lord," her mother was saying.

Lawrence never stopped gazing down at Louisa. It wasn't entirely certain he'd even heard her words.

"I don't know what's come over her," their mother said with a stilted, nervous laugh.

Lawrence wrapped a hand around her waist and his gaze was filled with unrestrained adoration as he squeezed her tightly against his side and addressed her mother. "Never apologize for Louisa," he said. "Certainly not to me."

"P-pardon me?" Her mother's voice was growing faint.

Either that, or Louisa was losing the ability to hear anything now that her heart was thumping wildly in her chest, her blood roaring in her ears at the sight of Lawrence's blatant affection—aimed at her and on full display.

Her mouth went dry as those blasted tears filled her eyes again. Why oh why did she turn into such a watering pot around this man?

"Torrent, did the present I asked for arrive?" he asked her father.

"Yes, yes. An unusual request, certainly," her father said with that same nervous laughter that her mother had used. "The servants left it in the ballroom upstairs as you requested."

Louisa arched her brows at him in silent question and his answering grin was outright mischievous.

She loved it.

"Come," he said, tugging her waist so she was falling into step beside him. "I have something to show you."

"But you mustn't," her mother called after them. "What about Margaret? She could go with you."

He paused in the doorway and Louisa was forced to turn back with him. She caught Margaret smothering a grin as their father pulled their mother to the side with a hurried "I shall explain everything to her" in Lawrence's direction.

Lawrence gave a curt nod. "You do that."

"What's going on?" her mother was saying as Lawrence started to turn with her still attached to his side. He was holding her so tight, like he might never let her go.

But then he stopped and threw a quick comment over his shoulder. It was directed to Margaret. "I have invited my friend Mr. Allen to join us for dinner this evening. I do hope that is all right."

"What? Oh, of course it is, but..." their mother was babbling a response but Lawrence and Louisa only had eyes for Margaret, and her smile was more genuine and heartfelt than any Louisa had ever seen from her sister in the past.

"You did that for her," Louisa whispered as they made their escape.

"I did it for them both," he said. "I have a suspicion that Gregory is just as smitten with your sister as I am with you."

"And now thanks to you and your generosity, Margaret can marry whomever she wishes," she said.

He gave a grunt of a laugh. "Please. I am hardly a selfless saint. Everything I did I did for you alone."

"Oh." She had no idea what to say to that and the moment they stepped into the empty ballroom, she forgot what she ought to say because she was too curious. "What are we doing up here?"

He steered her toward a painting that was covered in oilcloths. "I've spoken to your father..." He stopped and she stood before him, vibrating with tension and nerves and more excitement than she knew how to handle. His gaze turned earnest and oh-so-serious. "If it is amenable to you, my dear Louisa, I should very much like to ask for your hand—"

"Yes." She clamped her mouth shut in embarrassment. "Sorry, I ought to have let you finish."

He laughed before kissing her so thoroughly she forgot how to breathe. "Will you marry me?" he asked when he pulled back.

Now it was her turn to laugh. "Yes. Yes, yes, and yes!"

"First, I mean to court you," he informed her in that droll voice she loved so well. She loved that it covered up such deep emotions just as his stoic expression hid a fantastic wit and a lust for life and adventure that rivaled her own.

"Very well," she said, holding her arms out wide. "I am here to be courted."

He laughed. "But first I'd like to give you an early wedding present."

She looked down at the painting and back up in question.

"Rather than work out arrangements for a loan, I thought

it might be easier for your father to accept my money if I were purchasing something from him. So, in addition to the plot of land he was hoping to sell, I made him an offer on this painting...for you."

He removed the cloths and she started to laugh. "Sir Edmond!"

Lawrence shifted before her and for the first time she realized that he was just as excited and nervous and overcome by emotions as she was. She sighed melodramatically as she looked to the man who'd once been her ideal of all that was romantic.

She'd had no idea.

"Poor Sir Edmond," she said. "Do you think he'll be very heartbroken when he realizes he's been replaced in my heart by a living, breathing man?"

Lawrence grinned. "On the contrary. If he truly cares about you, he'd wish you all the happiness in the world. And if he can see all in his ethereal state, he'll know that the man you chose wants nothing so much as your happiness in life."

"Then poor Sir Edmond," she said as she leaned into his embrace. "But lucky me."

He kissed her long and tenderly before pulling back and adopting a pose for a waltz. "I thought Sir Edmond was an apt present to mark our betrothal," he said quietly as he moved in time to a silent melody only they could hear. "Do you know, up until I stepped into your arms that night, I felt rather like a ghost."

"No!" she said, tilting her head to the side. "How so?"

"My life had become terribly dull. Gray, even. The future was starting to look tedious, nothing more than obligations and duties. I was going through my days half asleep, taking my life for granted and focusing on all the things that did not matter."

She touched a hand to his cheek. "How sad."

"Isn't it, though?" He leaned down to kiss her. "But then I discovered you, and you...you *saved* me."

"I did?" she asked with delight.

"Yes, you took this ghost of a man and made him feel." He took one of her hands and placed it over his heart so she too could feel it pounding. "You made me feel, and you brought color and life into my gray existence." He stopped dancing to pull her in tightly. "You reminded me what it was to be alive. You showed me what it was to love. And now..." He rubbed his nose against hers. "And now I am so eager to see all the future has in store."

She leapt up suddenly, her toes dangling as she tackled him in an embrace. "You saved me too, you know. I never thought I'd meet anyone who loved me just as I am. I never thought I'd find someone who looked at me the way you do. Like I am truly special."

His arms wrapped around her tight. "Then perhaps we saved each other."

"You know, people will think you are crazy for choosing me."

She felt his grin against her cheek. "And they'll think you are insane for leaping into marriage with me."

She laughed. "Maybe we're both a little crazy then."

"Or maybe we both have faith. In love and in each other..."

"Faith," she repeated, pulling back to meet his gaze head on. "I like that. Marriage will be an adventure and this..." She pressed her hand to his heart again, feeling it leap with joy and love just as hers did. "*This* is a leap of faith."

## ABOUT THE AUTHOR

**MAGGIE DALLEN IS** the author of more than a hundred romantic comedies in a range of genres including young adult, historical, and contemporary. An unapologetic addict of all things romance, she loves to connect with fellow avid readers. Come say hello on Facebook or Instagram!

* 9 7 8 1 7 3 6 5 7 4 1 5 7 *

ND - #0385 - 270525 - C0 - 203/127/10 - PB - 9781736574157 - Matt Lamination